Earth's Only Paradise

Earth's Only Paradise

By

Polly McCanless Kent

Susan,

I hope my characters become as real to you as they are to me. I lived with so long they are special People to me. I hope you will feel that too.

Sincerely,
Polly Kent

ISBN: 0-75961-118-1

This book is printed on acid free paper.

1stBooks - rev. 2/22/01

Earth's Onely Paradise

By

Michael Drayton

Britains, you stay too long,
Quickly aboord bestow you
And with merry gale,
Swell your stretched sayle,
With vows as strong,
As the winds that blow you.

And cheerfully at sea,
Successe you still intice,
To get the pearle and gold,
And ours to hold,
Virginia,
Earth's Onely Paradise.

This book is dedicated to my husband BJ, who has supported me financially and emotionally throughout the whole process.

Background map in cover picture, courtesy of Christopher Stout, Webmaster@lincolnshire-web.co.uk
Original map by Captain John Smith

Girl in cover picture from a painting by Alexandra Lanford.

Chanco's Native American Philosophy from, "Wheel Of Life," by Howard Issac

April, 1616

Fate had given Payton Montgomery a push, and the decision had been made for him. It was time to seek his fortune in the new colony of Virginia.

There was one person in London who would be hurt if he left without a word. He would see her before he set sail on the morning tide. The hour was late but Angie had been like a sister to him since they were babes in Langley. Her father had been the caretaker of the Montgomery Estate and his father before him. She was probably just getting home from Blackfriars, where she was in charge of costumes for a Shakespearean play being performed there. A faint light from the window told him she was still up, so he knocked gently on her door.

Angie, in night clothes, greeted him joyfully at the door. Her Welch ancestors had given her the gift of beauty and intelligence, yet she had never appealed to him in more than a sisterly fashion. " Payton Montgomery, what are you doing on my doorstep at this time of the night; get yourself in here before my reputation is ruined."

"I came to tell you good-bye, Angie. I set sail for the Virginia Colony on the morn."

"Aye, so you are determined to get yourself killed for a piece of land on the other side of nowhere?"

"As second son, with only a pittance, I find myself with few options, Angie."

"Payton, you could take your choice of any lady in the whole of England. I hear how they swoon at your feet, the married and the single alike. 'Tis the adventure of it and your stubborn pride. I know you, Payton, better than you know yourself."

"Apparently you have heard about Father's young bride and the trouble her flirtations have caused."

"Aye, I heard, but I believed not a word of it. I know how you infuriate women with your honorable notions."

"I laid nary a finger on her and I think my Father knows that in his heart. He refuses to see the wench for what she is and he feels threatened by my presence there. He is extremely jealous of her and rightly so."

"Is that what sends you to the far corners of the earth to seek your fortune?'

"You know that I have been considering it ever since I heard John Rolfe give that talk at Cambridge. I've been fortunate in getting some good men at the cost of transporting them. I've even a Spaniard, bought his neck from the noose, I did. He is supposed to have some knowledge of raising tobacco, and it looks as if tobacco may become an important crop in the colony."

"Payton, why would you choose to break your back farming when you have the education to enter Parliament and do some good for the mother land?"

"Now, Angie, you've seen me back home working with the best of them. I enjoyed farming and I was good at it."

"Aye, you were a worker, Payton, and a good man to work under. Pa always said 'twas the wrong son came first."

"That's one reason I want to go to Virginia, Angie, I want to have a part in establishing a new system, one that allows any man the right to own anything he is willing to work for and the right to pass it down to the one he chooses."

"You always did try to change things, Payton, and you give every man his due. 'Tis not an easy task you speak of, for it is in every man to seek power and to want someone beneath him to lord it over. Maybe one day I will bring my new man and come see if you have made a difference in this new country."

"I've heard how the little shepherd's daughter from the North has taken London by storm with her costume designs. I also hear she has all the young gentlemen on their knees. I always knew you would make good if we could get you out where someone could see your work."

"You were the only one who had faith in me, Payton, and I want to thank you for it. 'Tis Shakespeare's plays that have brought notice to my costumes. Word from Stratford is that William's health is failing. 'Tis said his days are numbered. Such a man is he, to be able to see into the hearts and souls of the highest and the lowest of us. The more I hear his words, the more I see the wisdom contained in them." Angie looked pensive for a moment, then brightened. "Payton, I have a secret I am bursting to tell and I know it will be safe with you. Yesterday at two o'clock, in a private ceremony, I became Mrs. Samuel Arlington. He is a young gentleman of some standing in London. He hasn't told his family yet, but he soon will. We love each other so much, we are willing to face the outcome of such folly. He feels that after the initial blow, his father will be accepting of me. I can only pray it is so, for I would not want to separate him from his family. 'Tis not an absolute, but it is possible, that I am carrying his child. I have told this to no one, not even Samuel."

"Angie, I wish you every happiness. If I can put in a good word for you with the family, I will be happy to do so. You could contact me through any ship's captain, once I'm established in the colony. And now I must be on my way. The cock will soon be crowing and I only meant to say a quick good-bye."

Angie walked him to the door and as he opened it to leave, a fear grasped her heart that she might never see him again. She put out her arms and they embraced in innocent affection for a moment on the doorstep. Payton then put a finger beneath her chin and gave her a brotherly peck on the lips before turning to find a drunken Samuel Arlington standing halfway up the walk staring at them in pained confusion.

"I hope you are not going to let this man live to defame the honor of an Arlington, Sam. Have I not told you this woman is a doxy?" The young man who stood behind the drunken Samuel was deliberately trying to incite anger and he seemed to be sober.

"Sir, you have trampled on the honor of an Arlington. What do you have to say for yourself?" Sam asked with thick tongue.

ix

Payton and Angie tried to explain to Sam, but in his drunken state he was unreasonable. His cousin Robbie, laughing at them and telling Sam he was a fool to believe such a lame excuse, served to embolden Sam. He insisted on a duel, to be fought at dawn in a park by the river.

Payton, knowing he would be at sea by dawn and that the young man would either have sobered up to some sense or passed out to sleep it off, pretended to agree to the arrangements. He gave Angie a wink and noticed her relief as he walked to his buggy.

In Samuel's buggy, at the deserted park by the river, Robbie sat by his cousin, waiting. They had borrowed some pistols from a friend of Samuel's. Robbie had managed to keep Samuel drinking by reminding him that the woman he loved was unfaithful. He had planted explicit pictures of what had most likely taken place in her bedroom before he and Samuel had arrived to catch them on the doorstep.

As dawn lightened into daybreak, it became apparent that the man was not going to show. Robbie knew this was most likely his last chance to get rid of the cousin who stood between him and the Arlington fortune. He knew Samuel was very close to marrying the Welch fop, and once the seed of a legal son was planted his chance at the fortune would be gone.

Shaking Samuel from his drunken sleep, Robbie announced that the man had just arrived. Half carrying his cousin to a nearby tree, he ordered Samuel to stand against the tree, with pistol in hand, while Robbie stepped off the paces. When Robbie had walked about twenty paces from Samuel, he turned to find that Samuel had fallen and now lay on the ground, the pistol on the ground beside him. Walking back to Samuel with the second pistol in his hand, Robbie took his foot and rolled the unconscious Samuel onto his back. Robbie then took aim and shot him through the heart. Looking down at the body of his cousin, he found his shot had done the job even if a bit off from where he aimed. He would miss Samuel for Samuel was his only true friend. That was because Robbie had always been the poor cousin. Everything would change now.

Chapter One

August 3, 1621

Today Katherine would rid herself of Harvey Bland. For the better part of two years she had been courted by one milk sop after another, each handpicked by her stepfather. All were puppets in his plan to gain control of the inheritance that would go with her into marriage.

Katherine had arranged to have Harvey seated in the garden where the August heat and London humidity would soon wilt the ardor that brought on such spells of fawning and flattery. Now as Katherine made her way through the garden, she could see his fleshy body hobbling toward her on heels designed to make him appear taller. Trussed in garish suit, much slashed and with many loops and buttons at the slashes, he mopped his brow with a handkerchief of Danish lace. The sun caught the light of a large diamond on his hand, flashing from its bed of rubies. Katherine, caring little how she looked for this dreaded ordeal, and considering the heat, had left off the fashionable assemblage of petticoats. With fair hair tightly coiled and wearing a simple white lawn dress that fell softly to her ankles, her only thought was to getting this over and done.

"Katherine, you look like a Greek goddess today." Harvey extended a soft moist hand to her; the strong scent of musk and unclean body odors hung in the air around him. "The flowers of the garden fade in comparison to your beauty," he continued.

"Harvey, we must talk seriously today," Katherine replied, wrenching her hand from his and sidestepping the scent.

"I too am bursting with the joyous news. I see Mr. Barlow has told you of our decision."

"No, he has told me nothing," she said.

"He has not told you that we are to be wed? Your stepfather and I have come to an agreement and he has given his permission. My mother was rather put out by the terms, but Mr.

1

Barlow came around last night and persuaded her to see things our way. Now that it is settled, Mother has begun making the arrangements. Mr. Barlow explained your mother's condition and asked Mother to take care of the formalities. Although, I must admit, we haven't given her much time for the preparations."

Shock, followed by a draining weakness, swept through Katherine. Finding a nearby garden stool, she sank onto it in silence while Harvey chatted on about his pleasure in taking her as his wife, saying he had been unable to sleep all night contemplating the beauty that would be his to ravish at will. When he mentioned that the wedding was to be a quiet little affair that would take place in a month, Katherine jumped to her feet in a burst of indignation. "Harvey, listen to me, I know nothing of such an agreement, there will be no wedding."

"What are you saying, my dear? Of course there will be a wedding. Mr. Barlow is your legal guardian and he has given his word. You have no choice in the matter." The expression on his face became that of a spoiled child being refused something already in hand.

"I do not love you and I could never be a wife to you, Harvey."

"That will come later; you will see how quickly I can arouse passion in you, given some time alone. I have experience in these things. I can make you happy, Katherine, I know I can." His voice had now changed to a plea.

"My stepfather is using us both to get at my inheritance. I will not allow him to use me. I would respect you more if you refused also."

"Oh, no, you are wrong about him, Katherine. He intends to protect you and me by retaining a full partnership in the shipping firm and helping me to build it up with the money from your trust."

"A shipping firm that he has milked dry. A prosperous business it was before he got his hands in the till," she answered, then turned to go.

"I want you, Katherine. I find you more desirable than any woman I have ever known." With that he grabbed her and spun her around; his lips came down on hers in a wet smothering kiss that made her stomach turn. His arms, now around her, had both her arms pinned to her sides. Katherine could only turn her face away while he slobbered all over her cheek. When he stuck his tongue in her ear, she brought up her knee as a wedge to push away his sweaty body, but as her knee came up it made contact with his groin. With a gasp he let her go, and doubled over in pain. Looking up in chafed surprise, Harvey saw that her eyes, usually a soft warm green, had become cold as ice. He was reminded of the hearth cat he had once touched with a hot poker. On impulse she slapped his face, "I will never marry you," she spat. "I would die before I would let you touch me again."

Katherine turned and marched toward the house, leaving Harvey to recover from the sting of her handprint on his face and the pain that throbbed in his groin

While Mr. Barlow was eating his lunch, Roberta Wiggins had come to tidy up the library that served as his study. She had worked her way to the back shelves and was just finishing up when Mr. Barlow and the Widow Bland entered and closed the door behind them. Roberta wondered what the two of them were up to, as they had only recently become acquainted.

"I'm pleased with the arrangements you have made so far, my dear," Roberta heard Mr. Barlow say. " We will get the two of them married, and in the meantime perhaps I will be able to become more intimately acquainted with the mother of the groom."

Roberta could hardly believe her ears, Mr. Barlow talking in such a tone as to lead the poor soul on while his own wife lay in a drugged stupor in the room over their heads. Stout and plain the Widow Bland was, at least a dozen years older in age, twenty years older in looks.

She heard the widow giggle, then, "Thomas, you devil. You know a lady of my position can't be seen carrying on with a married gentleman, even if his wife is on her deathbed."

3

"I know that a lady of your passion and intelligence can find a way to fulfill any desires she may have." Mr. Barlow answered in a voice dripping with suggestion. A rustle of the widow's gowns led Roberta to believe that an embrace had taken place. She was shocked at Mr. Barlow taking advantage of a lonely old widow, then wondered why she would be shocked at anything he did after the way he had deceived Lady Arlington. Must be something in it for him, she thought. Then, as if in answer to her thoughts, she heard him become his old self again.

"Now, my dear, let's get back to the business at hand. This is the contract for Harvey to sign. It merely states that the money in Katherine's trust will be turned over to the shipping firm of which I will remain, upon their marriage and the release of her funds, a full partner. If all is agreeable with Harvey, my barrister will come by on Friday morning at ten to acknowledge the signature."

"Harvey is so enamored of Katherine's beauty, he would sign anything. You still don't know the exact amount of her trust?"

"No, but even with accrued interest, I doubt that it is more than a mere pittance in comparison with the great wealth left to Harvey by his father. The bulk of Mr. Arlington's fortune will go to his nephew Robbie to maintain the Arlington estates, due to the sad fact that there are no male heirs in this branch of the family. Ah, but you are not to worry about Katherine's trust. With my knowledge of shipping and the capital provided by her trust fund, we can take advantage of the expansion of commerce to our new colonies in America. I foresee this to be a profitable investment for Harvey and myself as well. It is no small comfort to me, knowing that I will have an enterprising young son-in-law to turn it all over to when I retire. Well, dear, you take the contract and get Arthur to bring around your carriage. I see Katherine coming up from the garden in a rush. I would guess that Harvey has broken the news to her and that we will have some things to discuss alone."

"Thomas, you won't forget that Katherine's to be at the dressmaker's tomorrow at two to be fitted for her trousseau?"

4

"I will be out of town on business until late Thursday, but I will arrange for her to be there. If you would, come by with Harvey on Friday to act as a witness. Afterwards, we can take a ride out into the country. Until then, dear."

Roberta could see him guiding the widow toward the front entrance, away from the door Katherine would use to come in from the garden. She knew there would not be time to slip out before he returned, so she pulled up a stool near an empty space on the shelves, which gave her a view of the room from a slant so that she would not be seen. No sooner had Mr. Barlow gotten back to his seat behind the desk than Katherine came bursting through the doors.

"How dare you, you have no right to make such arrangements without my permission. Under no circumstances will I marry that blubbering fool, or for that matter any of the spineless creatures you persist in pushing off on me. Do you understand me, Mr. Barlow?"

Roberta could see the cold fury in Katherine's eyes and was reminded of Katherine's father, Matthew Arlington, when she had seen him angry.

"From this day forth I will be plagued by no more of the fawning idiots you allow through the gates. You will find that I am not like my mother, Mr. Barlow. I will not lie down and give up. I know the terms of my father's will. If married, I could have received my inheritance at eighteen and as English law dictates, it would have become property of my husband. This is the only reason you have taken such an interest in my suitors. One year from this September, when I am twenty-one, I will receive my inheritance, married or not. Until that time I will receive no more gentlemen callers unless they are of my own choosing."

Mr. Barlow, having regained his tongue after the unexpected outburst, now stood behind his desk with assurance. "My dear spoiled stepchild, I have given you almost two years to choose a husband. As you pass the prime of womanhood it will become harder and harder to find a suitable match. Therefore, I have

5

taken matters into my own hands, as I have every right to do. You will marry Harvey Bland as arranged. I have already spoken to your mother, and she upholds me in my decision to see you settled into a good marriage with a prominent gentleman of considerable wealth. The matter is closed, so go to your room and do not come out until you have accepted what your elders have decided is best for a young lady of your age and position."

"You know that Mother has chosen to obliterate herself from the misery of being married to you through ever increasing doses of laudanum, which you obtain for her. In her right mind, she would not want me married to someone I detest. I will never marry Harvey Bland or any other man that you use to get at my inheritance. I would as soon roast in hell." With shoulders back and head high she walked out into the hall and up the stairs to her room.

The scene between Mr. Barlow and Katherine had left Roberta shaken. She was very much afraid for the girl, alone in the world except for distant relatives in the North and a mother who was powerless to save her own self from this man. Katherine had, during the worst of times, showed strength of character, still she was a poor match for Mr. Barlow. Mr. Arlington had been mistaken to raise her in such a way that she did not know her place as a woman. Filling her head with all that education, that French girls' school, and making too much over her. Treated her like a son he had. Now 'twas the girl who had to suffer for it. Women were to serve the needs of men and bear children; the sooner Katherine learned that, the better off she would be. Roberta feared too that Katherine had come under the wrath of God. She had always been a good and loving child, but after she came home from France she often read books that questioned God's very words and she made shocking comments about the clergy. After the death of her father, Katherine had committed blasphemy. The words Katherine had said to Reverend Gates as he had tried to comfort her were burnt into Roberta's mind. "From this day forth I renounce a God who metes out punishment and reward at random. If there is indeed a

God, there must be laws and principles by which He abides and I will seek to understand them. Not through pious men who stand between us and God, but through humble teachers who show us the way to a direct and personal relationship with our creator." Roberta had prayed that the Lord would not strike Katherine dead in that moment and had prayed for her forgiveness every day since. She prayed now that Katherine was not getting ready to face a reckoning for her blasphemy, reminding God that the child had suffered more than was her share of death and sorrow.

Roberta was impatient to get out of the study. The other servants would soon miss her, and things were piling up that needed her attention. Instead of leaving, Mr. Barlow rang the bell and Maggie came to the study, wiping her hands on her apron. "Send Giles in and be quick about it," Mr. Barlow snapped.

"Yes, sire." Maggie sensed his wrath and hurried to do his bidding.

Giles was a servant brought along by Mr. Barlow when he had married Mrs. Arlington. A vile man, he was always sneaking around, listening for something to run and report to his master. The other servants despised and feared him. A word from him could bring dismissal, and jobs were scarce in these times.

Giles came in, hat in hand, then stepped back to close the door at a signal from Mr. Barlow.

"I have to be away on business for a day or two, and I would like you to keep an eye on Katherine. She may get it in her head to run off to avoid marrying Harvey Bland. She has to be at the dressmaker's at two o'clock tomorrow afternoon. Afterwards, see that she goes nowhere or talks to no one outside the house. If she hasn't come around to my way of thinking by the time I return, perhaps some disciplinary action will bring her down off her high horse."

A perverse light flickered in Giles' eyes at Mr. Barlow's suggestion.

7

"Yes, sire, ye can trust ole Giles, sire, she won't get out of me sight. Ye can count on that."

"Go now and saddle Prince for me. On horseback I can make this trip in haste and get back to this business with Katherine."

"I'll see to Prince this minute sire, and don't you worry none about the Lady Katherine, I'll see to her, I will."

As soon as Giles had left, Mr. Barlow put the papers on his desk into a briefcase and left the study. Roberta could hear his footsteps on the stairs when she stepped quietly into the hall. Breathing a sigh of relief, she made her way out to the kitchen.

"That incorrigible rogue," she thought, "driving poor Mrs. Arlington to her grave with his cruelty and his squandering of her fortune. Now he has his black heart set on getting Miss Katherine's inheritance. A pittance, he had told Widow Bland; he knew better than that. Pulling the wool over her eyes, same as he had done with Katherine's mother. Oh, he was a sly one when it came to women. 'Twould do her heart good to see him thwarted by Miss Katherine, but she could see no possible way for this to happen, unless the Lord provided a miracle.

The miracle, or what Roberta assumed to be a miracle, was waiting for Roberta in the servants' mail. It was a letter from Jenny Lawrence, the daughter of Mrs. Arlington's older sister Hannah. Jenny had been disowned years ago because she had run away to marry a ship's mate. Every year or two she would write to Roberta, begging for news of the family. According to the letter, Jenny was ill and had taken to her bed. Of all the relatives who came to mind, Jenny was the one most likely to be sympathetic of Katherine's predicament and would welcome her company. Jenny also offered the safest place for Katherine to stay until she could claim her inheritance. Roberta felt sure that Mr. Barlow had never heard of Jenny Lawrence.

Chapter 2

Back in her room, Katherine paced the floor in dismay. The elation of having spoken her mind to Mr. Barlow had now worn off, and she was faced with the problem of carrying out her threats. She had gone to her mother's room, but had found her incoherent. Having very little money of her own until she came of age left Katherine with no solution she could think of. She could go to her father's people in the North, but they would have little sympathy for her. They married their own daughters off in the same manner, always with an eye to increasing their wealth or power. In frustration, Katherine burst into tears and started to beg God for help, then remembered she had sworn that she would never go begging to God again. Although the God and the truths that she had been seeking her whole life were undefined, she intuitively perceived that begging was not the expected approach.

A soft knock on her door brought Katherine out of this frustrating mental process. She opened it to the pale drawn face of Roberta.

"Katherine, if ye be bound and determined not to marry this Harvey Bland, then ye must leave and be quick about it." Roberta then told her what she had heard in the library. "I have just received a letter from yer first cousin Jenny Lawrence. Roberta explained to Katherine who Jenny was and why she could not remember her. "Jenny never offered to come around the family. She has through the years written to me for news. Ye must go to her for she is the only one who will understand your plight. Her husband died a few years back, leaving her comfortable in a home of her own. She remained childless and her health is failing. 'Twould be good for her to have ye there. 'Twas a good child, she was, in spite of the disgrace she brought to the family. Ye often put me in mind of Jenny yerself, ye both are inclined to be headstrong."

9

"How do you plan for me to get to this cousin, that may or may not want me? You said that Giles was supposed to prevent me from leaving."

"The Widow Bland has set ye up an appointment for a trousseau fitting with Clara at two o'clock tomorrow afternoon. The coach to Plymouth leaves at three: I know, for me own sister Bessie always takes it to Aldershot. Giles has been ordered not to let ye out of his sight, so when he thinks ye safely set at the dressmaker's, then Arthur will pick ye up in the alley behind Clara's shop and see ye to the coach. The minute ye leave the house, Arthur will load up ye trunks and follow. As soon as ye git to the shop, ye must feign a sudden illness or a need to relieve yerself; ye will be shown to the chamber in the back where ye can slip out. Arthur will be waiting in ye brother Samuel's old buggy. Now, child, ye must be out by half past two in order to make the coach."

"Are you saying that I am to travel all the way to Plymouth without a chaperone?"

"I will be sick with worry over you traveling alone. Arthur has come to know the driver from taking me sister Bessie so many times and will ask him to see after ye. 'Tis the only thing we can do that won't draw notice. I feared ye might go off half cocked on ye own. I prayed to the good Lord for a miracle and there was the letter, seemed like a sign, it did. 'Tis said that Plymouth is a cold and windy place. Mind ye pack with an eye to practicality. I aim to git some stuff together to send to Jenny, a bit of spices that are hard to come by and herbs to ease her infirmity."

Giles hovered near her door as Katherine spent the rest of the afternoon going through her clothes and laying aside those which seemed appropriate. In the end she found her wardrobe sadly lacking. Mr. Barlow had only allowed her to purchase clothing for the fancy affairs that he set up for her. At dinner a picture of her mother in the dining hall dressed in country attire reminded Katherine of the fine country clothes in her mother's trunks.

10

Going straight to her mother's chamber, Katherine shut the door in Giles' face and approached her mother again. Her dinner tray sat untouched by her bed; she slept soundly. Katherine shook her gently and could feel her come awake, at least as much as she could under the influence of the laudanum. "Mother may I please talk to you? It is very important." Marie Arlington's eyelids fluttered and she smiled a weak smile.

"Hello, dear, of course you may talk to me. I was dreaming of your father just then. If only he hadn't died. Our life would be so different. It was only through him that I was able to bear the death of our dear Sam. When Matthew died, he may as well have taken me with him. At least you have John to look after you. Is it true that he has found a husband for you, or did I dream it?"

"Oh, Mother," Katherine sobbed, "I am so thankful to find you able to talk tonight. Mr. Barlow has devised a scheme to get the money that Father left for me in the trust fund. He has finally found a man willing to sign it over to him, a man whom I would rather die than marry. If you will get off the laudanum and stand up to him, I won't have to go away and leave you. I am so afraid to leave you with him. Oh please, Mother, you are going to die if you don't stop taking that tincture that Mr. Barlow brings you. Look how thin you have gotten." ·

"Why, darling, you don't know what you are saying, your mother is very ill and that medicine is the only thing keeping me alive. I'm sure John knows what is best for all of us, you must trust him dear. He would never do anything to hurt you. You must stop all this talk of going away: you are all I have left except for John. Now, dear, you must leave me for it is time for my medicine."

"Mother, where are your riding clothes? I thought perhaps I might borrow something from them to go riding tomorrow."

Her mother looked up at her for the first time in months.

"Katherine, you have turned into an elegant young lady, so refined and trim now, perhaps my clothes would fit you. Take anything you like, they are packed in the trunks in the nursery.

11

Come back and talk to me tomorrow, we will talk about your wedding."

Marie Arlington had loved their country estate and had spent much time there. Among her clothes were warm night rails, shoes of buff leather, and clothes of classic design. The fabrics were more suitable to everyday wear. Katherine knew that soon as August was over, the winds coming in from the ocean would be cool. She chose sturdy gowns of lustrous homespun linen, dimity, and warm wool. There were foreparts and petticoats of silk tabby, striped linen, worsted, and prunella. It was near midnight when Katherine shook the sleeping Giles and asked him to help her carry a large trunk of clothes down to the back hall for Arthur to take to the church poor. She explained that she was trying to take care of a few things before she became involved with the wedding.

Directly after the morning meal, preserves, spices, and herbs were packed into Katherine's trunk in the downstairs hall. By midday another trunk sat beside it. Arthur was able to get them loaded onto Sam's buggy while Giles was eating his midday meal.

Roberta then informed Giles of Mr. Barlow's orders that Katherine be taken to the dressmaker at half past one, acting as if he didn't know. Given the amount of brandy that Roberta had allowed him to pour into his cup after the meal, she was sure he would nap in the carriage as soon as he left Katherine at the dress shop.

Katherine had spent part of the morning composing a letter to be taken to Arnold Dunbar, her father's barrister. He had been a friend of the family for years, especially since the death of her father. She informed him of her intention to stay in hiding until her twenty-first birthday and the receipt of her trust fund. She explained that conditions with her stepfather had become intolerable. She warned him that Mr. Barlow would use any means to get at her inheritance and that he was to allow him nothing. She told him to notify her cousin Robbie and tell him he could take possession of the Arlington estate at any time, respecting of course her father's stipulation that her mother would always have a home there. She asked that Robbie allow the servants to stay until she returned, for they were like family, and her mother needed those who were familiar to her.

Robbie had always loved her mother, and she hoped he would insure the safety of her mother while she was gone. She smiled at the thought of Mr. Barlow having to give up his position as head of the house. In reference to a letter she had recently received from Mr. Dunbar concerning the settlement of the estate of her Great Aunt Katherine Leigh Randolph, for whom Katherine had been named, she wrote her instructions. Her aunt's small house in London had been left to Katherine, and it needed some immediate repairs. Katherine authorized him to take money from her allowance and have the repairs made, as she would need the house on her return to London. In the event that her servants were put out with no place to go, she asked that he put them up in the small house and continue to pay their wages from the funds provided for them. Living arrangements were for Roberta and Arthur; Cooke Della and Maggie preferred living in their own homes. Arthur would deliver the letter as soon as she was settled on the Plymouth coach.

When Katherine arrived for her appointment at Clara's shop, there was much ado over the wedding of a nobleman's daughter, and they were running late for her appointment. This made it easy for her to slip away unnoticed. Arthur was waiting in the alley.

Katherine had not been in her brother's buggy since his death five years ago. Arthur had kept it clean and shined, for it had been prized by her brother Sam. Sitting on the rich leather seats, she remembered the times that he would take her to her childhood activities and tease her about growing into a comely young lady. She remembered how proud she was to be seen with him, and she missed him with a deep longing. If only he hadn't got himself killed in that silly duel. Perhaps Mother would have taken Father's death better and never have married Mr. Barlow. Sam had always been her mother's heart and she

13

her father's. Katherine remembered the hidden compartment that Sam had ordered to be made into the divider that framed the middle of the seat facing forward. The divider, he had explained proudly, added a supportive handrail to the passenger on rough roads, while also keeping valuables safely hidden in the event of robbery. Katherine flipped the catch that opened the padded arm and lifted it up. She was surprised to find a folded sheet of paper inside, yellowed by age. She unfolded the official looking paper and noticed it was dated two days before his death. At the top it said Certificate of Marriage. Katherine was puzzled and intrigued as she read Samuel's name and that of a girl named Angela Mellon. By this time they had reached the Post, so she hurriedly folded it and returned it to the secret compartment.

At the posthouse Katherine paid her fare while Arthur saw to the loading of her trunks. An elderly man and woman sat side by side in the coach awaiting the last minute details of driver and footmen. Katherine was helped into the seat facing them. Arthur then went to have a word with the driver, who had recognized him with a wave. The sweet, grandmotherly lady smiled at Katherine and began to make small talk, putting Katherine at ease about traveling alone. The driver soon whipped the horses and Arthur waved farewell as the coach jolted away.

Katherine's traveling companions were a couple from Plymouth. They introduced themselves as Mr. and Mrs. Baley and said they had been in London a fortnight on business. Mrs. Baley was friendly and talkative, but Mr. Baley sat with sour face and barely grunted when Mrs. Baley asked for a response from him. Something about the way he looked at Katherine when he thought she wasn't looking made her wary of him. Not wishing to go into detail about her affairs, she told Mrs. Baley her name was Katherine Lawrence and she was traveling to Plymouth to attend an ailing cousin. Mrs. Baley said she had heard of Katherine's cousin, Jenny, but did not know her personally.

14

The women chatted in the dusty, jolting coach until late evening when they finally stopped in Aldershot for supper and a short wait for the driver and horses which would take them on to Plymouth. It was dark when the passengers boarded the coach again, and Katherine pretended to sleep. Mrs. Baley's curiosity and pointed questions had led Katherine to say much more than she had intended about her affairs. She was sure the lady was just curious, but her questions had begun to pry, putting Katherine on guard. Now she wished to avoid further inquiry. The road was rough and the coach lurched so that sleep was impossible until the predawn hours when exhaustion and a smoother road made it possible to sleep a few moments at a time.

Shortly after dawn the coach stopped at Yoevil and the passengers took a morning meal before setting out on the last leg of their journey. Here they were joined by another woman traveling alone, not the kind who would concern herself over the propriety of such action. The road was rough and the coach lurched so that Katherine and the woman named Marjorie were constantly being thrown against each other. After an hour or so they gave up trying not to touch each other and began to laugh about it. Katherine found herself liking the woman in spite of her street manner and indecent apparel. Just before noon the coach reached Plymouth, and Marjorie hurried off down the street toward the waterfront. Katherine accepted a ride with the Baley's to their tavern, where she freshened up and partook of a midday meal. As promised the matron had a carriage brought up for Katherine to be taken the few miles out to Cherry Lane where her cousin resided. The matron had taken the driver aside to give whispered instructions while Katherine was eating, and now she bid Katherine good-bye and invited her to stop in for a visit once she was settled.

It seemed they had gone only a short distance when the driver pulled up in front of a modest house that was apparently deserted. The windows were boarded up and the grounds had not recently been tended. The driver pounded on the door for several minutes before giving up and returning to the carriage.

15

"Wot now Miss?" he asked.

"Return to the Baley's tavern and I will take a room there while I inquire as to my cousin. I fear she may have taken a turn for the worse."

It was almost as if Mrs. Baley had expected her return: a room had been made ready and Katherine's baggage taken to it before she had a chance to explain her reason for returning. When she voiced her plans to inquire as to her cousin through the town doctor and the postal service, Mrs. Baley insisted the carriage driver be sent to make the inquiries.

Mrs. Bailey showed Katherine to her room, where she had warm milk waiting so that Katherine might take a short rest before dinner. As soon as Katherine drank the milk, she became engulfed in a fatigue that she assumed was due to the tiring journey. Possessing not the inclination or the energy to undress herself, Katherine slumped onto the bed and fell asleep, while Mrs. Baley fussed with the details of having water brought up and so forth.

Katherine awoke to pitch-black darkness and a penetrating dampness that chilled her to the bone. The strong smell of beer mingled with that of urine and unclean bodies. With a foggy slowness, she began to come to her senses. With consciousness came the realization that she was moving swiftly through the water on a vessel of some sort. Listening, she began to notice the sounds of rhythmic breathing coming from all around her.

"Where am I?" she asked with a tongue that felt swollen and dry. Her thoughts were fuzzy.

"Miss, you have been drugged and abducted. On yer way ye are to the Royal Colony of Virginia, holed up 'tween decks with the rest of us." The rough voice came from a woman on her right.

"How long have I been here?" Katherine asked.

Again from her right, "'Tis past midnight. Wot do ye last remember?"

"It was just past midday. Mrs. Baley gave me some warm milk."

"At old crow, she'd sell 'er own mother. Lining her pockets with gold she is, selling maidens fer indentures or wives, giving nary a thought to the fate and families of them girls. They say she's being watched. They'll have her head on the block the first wrong move she makes, and ye just might be that. Gads, ye must be sumpthin' special. The captain delivered ye here hisself. Handling ye like gold, he was, and followed by them fancy trunks. Said ye was worth more than the lot of us put together and threatened us with a lashing if we so much as touched any of ye belongings. Said ye had to have all the trappings of a lady when we got to Virginia, fer ye were being delivered to a fine gentleman, and was ye that would make this trip worthwhile."

"You said 'us'; how many more are here?" Katherine asked.

"Ten besides yeself, two more abducted but not of yer quality. Most of us got no place better to go. A few of us willing to go anywhere to escape the beatings of husbands or the ravishes of masters. 'Tis a sad lot ye've been throwed in with, Miss. Most of us, we're used to hardship, but you, I got me doubts ye ever make it across this bloody ocean."

"What's your name?" Katherine asked the woman.

"Doris is what me mama named me, but I been called by so many since, I hardly know me name anymore."

"Well, Doris, my name is Katherine and I have sailed many times; doubt not that I will make it across this ocean and back home again."

17

Chapter 3

Katherine had never been one to get seasick, but having been brought aboard in a drugged state to sail into high winds and rough seas, was enough to purge the stomach of an able seaman. The first three days out found Katherine rushing often to the rail with a stomach that rolled and tossed with the ship. The wind at the rail bathed her body in a coolness that brought a few moments' relief before the nausea set in again. Were it not for the weakness of her body, she would have stayed there against the rail to savor the chill of the wind in her face. She knew the danger of being on deck in such turbulent seas, especially in a weakened state. Sick as Katherine was, some of the girls who had never sailed were much sicker, and a very young girl called Charlotte had not risen from her pallet since the first day out. Sometime in the predawn hours of the fourth day Katherine awoke from a restless sleep to find the ship moving through smooth waters, and the nausea subsided. The retching had left her sore and weak, and she knew her recovery depended upon getting something to stay down that could quickly strengthen. Among the gifts that Roberta had packed for Cousin Jenny were fruit preserves; she forced herself up and searched through her trunks to find them. In the stink and clutter of the mess around them, Katherine found dirty spoon, mug, and the bucket of water which they had learned to avoid for it brought on more retching.

Stirring a spoon of preserves into a half cup of water, she sipped slowly until it was gone and streaks of dawn broke on the horizon. Awakening the other girls, she made some of them drink from the mug also, and by midday all but Charlotte were on their feet again. Sometime during the worst of her illness Katherine could recall Charlotte moaning and crying, but Katherine had been unable to worry about anything but getting to the rail and back. Now as they moved toward evening of that fourth day Katherine again approached the child with her cup of watered down sweetness. Putting her hand on the girl, she could feel the fever and called to the others to bring pan and water to cool her searing brow. As three of the more congenial of the girls came to help, they decided to remove clothing and bathe the whole of her fevered body. Katherine let out a gasp as she raised a gown to find the girl lying in a mass of blood-soaked underclothes. "Oh my God, she's dying," Katherine exclaimed.

One of the women whom Katherine suspected as being a woman of the streets, came to look at the unconscious girl, then turned to Katherine with a look of unconcern. "'Tis a baby, Miss. The girl has lost a baby and 'tis likely better for the both of 'em, allowing the fever don't git 'er."

"What can we do for the poor child?" Katherine asked.

"If we could git 'er on 'er feet to keep the flow going. Tis said the bits and pieces of the babe can rot in the womb and bring on the fever."

"This child is not able to stand, what else could we do?"

"All's I know, Miss, is drag 'er up and make 'er walk. I just 'eard of the fever, don't know wot ye do fer it."

Katherine forced some of the sweetened water into the girl's mouth while calling her name. With gentle shakes and slaps she got the pretty child to respond. "Charlotte, this will give you some strength so we can get you up. You have lost your baby. Now we must get you up and keep the flow going so your body can rid itself of the aborted tissue; otherwise you could get the fever and die."

"'Twould be a blessing Miss," the girl whispered weakly. "Were it not for burning in hell, I would that I had gone with the cursed babe."

"You are not going to die, child. I am going to see to it that you don't. A loving God would never hold a beloved child like yourself accountable for any man's sin. Put to rest your thoughts of hell. Now let's get you out of those bloody rags and into these warm flannels, for you are chilled to the bone."

"You are a beautiful lady, Miss." Charlotte told her a few days later, "Was an angel I thought ye were when first ye roused me from the sickness."

"I don't think you realize what a beautiful woman you will be, given another year or two. Perhaps it will work out that I can take you to live with me. It would give me great comfort to have a friend with me in this new world, and you need time for healing, child, after all that you have been through."

Charlotte had told Katherine of her mother's brother, who had raped her two years ago and continued to use her since. When she realized she was pregnant and told that he was the father, her uncle accused her of being a witch that had mesmerized him. The wife of the uncle had kept the village stirred up until there was talk of burning Charlotte at the stake. Her father believed her to be an innocent victim, but feared for her life with such talk going around their small village; therefore, he had arranged for her to be put on the ship for America.

As a distraction to the long days aboard ship, Katherine began to teach Charlotte her letters. She suggested that she learn enough to write her parents in her own hand to let them know that the baby had been lost and that she was recovering nicely. It would relieve their mind a bit, for they would surely worry about her.

Captain Jamison, by this time having heard of the miscarriage and of Katherine taking the girl under her wing, asked that Katherine be brought before him. Following a crew member to his quarters, Katherine was shown into the tidy cabin that served as office and living quarters for the staunch, bearded man who sat behind a desk. Asking the crewman to leave and shut the door, the captain cleared his throat and began. "Miss Lawrence, word of the goings on below deck has reached my ears, and since it is past time that I talk with you concerning your future, I have called you forth. My intention upon arrival in the Colony of Virginia, is to sell you to a gentleman who is known to desire a lady of some breeding. The gentleman, Payton Montgomery, is a man of high moral character, and it is possible he would refuse to take you if he knew the circumstances that put you there. Therefore, I have brought you here to explain that in purchasing you and your baggage from the Baleys, I have saved you from a fate worse than death. Because you are a blond and comely lass with an air of fineness about you, a trader could name his price and get it in the East. 'Tis custom among the men of wealth in the East to keep a harem of love slaves. Drawn are they to the fair and blond, willing to trade high in valuable silks and spices for one with your countenance. Should you choose not to cooperate in this matter, I will be forced to trade or sell you in order to recover my investment. In which case I would guess that you would still be sold in the East, for 'tis there the greatest profit is found. I do not like the idea of sending a lady to such a fate and would prefer that you accept a man of your own country and customs."

"Captain Jamison, I understand your position, but I can make no decision until I see this man and decide how I feel about being married to him. There are some men over whom I would choose death, such as the man I fled when kidnaped by the Baleys." Katherine, having noticed that Captain Jamison had called her Miss Lawrence, wondered if being married under the false name of Lawrence could make marriage to the Virginia gentleman illegal. Even though it was likely that she would come out of it as damaged goods, it would give her some comfort to know she could get out of such a marriage.

"'Tis also a mixed bag of women with whom you travel," Captain Jamison said, breaking into her thoughts "I would ask that ye refrain from exposing yeself to the diseases and poxes that are sure to be among these women."

"That is something I wish to talk to you about. The filth and stink of our quarters is unbearable, and new knowledge points to cleanliness as the most effective measure against disease. I would like your permission, sir, to have saltwater drawn for washing and cleaning."

"Permission granted, Miss Lawrence, as long as you don't take my men away from their duties. I will see that they keep water for ye, but that will be the extent of their help. Now I must get to my ledgers."

21

When next Captain Jamison appeared on deck, he was flabbergasted to find that clothes and bedclothes flapped from every available line of mast and rigging. "I pray this mass washing will soon be taken in," he told Katherine, "it is impossible for my crew to carry out their duties with wet clothes slapping them in the face at every turn." He paced the deck for a while, dodging the women who seemed to be everywhere hunting a place to hang more dripping clothes; then he took refuge in his cabin.

The lookout, a cheerful Irish lad, was enjoying his view of the washing and yelling jokingly to his crew members. "They's room for one more bodice in the mizzen ratlines. Yo, Jenks, see to that pair of drawers on the stern deck, they's bout to blow away." Thus the novelty of the women's washing broke the humdrum after days at sea and distracted the crew. It's no wonder the other ship was within cannon range before anyone noticed.

Captain Jamison was out on deck with red face when the English shallop, the Merry Maid, came alongside. As it drew near the men aboard could be seen on the rails, bent double in laughter. "Ho there, Captain, we been trying to make out the nationality of this ship for more than an hour," the Captain of the Merry Maid yelled between cupped hands. "Had not the wind changed directions and moved a corset aside so the flag could be seen, we might have blown ye out of the water and killeth our own countrymen. Some say maybe ye be Spanish; others say no, the Spanish never wash their stynking clothes. Some say maybe 'tis an international whore boat to serve men on the high seas; others say, no, too many of them Puritans on the water these days. Tell me Captain of the, let's see, brush aside those lacy stockings, ah the Marmaduke. What the hell are ye doing out here looking like a floating rag peddler?"

"'Tis a load of women I take to the colonies. We started out with rough seas and some of them didn't come through smelling too fresh. One of 'em talked me into letting them have a housecleaning. Didn't figure on something like this when I agreed."

The Merry Maid was on its way home after months of being at sea. Captain Jamison was invited over so they could trade news, and for an hour or so the visit got him out of the flapping clothes.

By suppertime the clothes had been taken in. Though stiff and rough from the saltwater and lye soap, they brought the scent of ocean breezes and sunshine to the scoured quarters.   As the days turned into weeks the women settled into life aboard the ship, growing accustomed to the cracking of canvas and the creaking of the hull as it broke water. With familiarity came routine, then boredom and irritability. There was constant bickering among the women. The cramped quarters, meal after meal of salt pork, and the limited amount of activity all contributed to the worsening of the situation. Into their second month at sea, violent fights were not uncommon. The less aggressive of the group sank into melancholy. Tension hung like a thick gray fog over the ship.

This being Captain Jamison's first voyage with a shipload of women, he was at his wit's end as to what to do about their fighting. A few of the women had begun to amuse themselves with his men, causing fights and hard feelings among them also. On deck he came upon Katherine, book in hand, teaching Charlotte to read and write. At his suggestion Katherine began holding classes everyday, as soon as the morning meal was cleared away in the galley. In order to get the women's attention she began by reading to them from the books of poetry which she had packed for her trip to her cousin's. One of the poems she read to them was a merry ballad written by Michael Drayton to cheer the first colonists to Virginia in 1606. The ballad predicted, "pearle and gold, and ours to hold, Virginia, Earth's Onely Paradise."   Using something different each day to gain their attention, Katherine then proceeded to teach them first the spelling and writing of their own names and then moved on to the recognition of simple words that she printed on paper given to her by Captain Jamison.

Sensing their interest in the Virginia Colony and feeling an interest herself, Katherine asked Captain Jamison to come and give a talk on what the women could expect when they got there. Through a copy of George Percy's, "Observations," loaned to Katherine by the captain, the women had learned, "of noble forests with carpets of flowers and strawberries foure times bigger and better than England's." From journals and other writings they had learned of, "Indians creeping on all fours from the hills, like bears, with their bows in their mouths to attack the settlers," of "cruel diseases such as swellings, fluxes and burning fevers," of "famine that left bodies trailing from cabins like dogs to be buried." But these were all experiences that applied to a different time and to different people. What the women wanted from Captain Jamison was to know what was going to happen to them, from the time they arrived to the time he left them there.

"As ye know," Captain Jamison began, "the purpose of this trip is to provide the settlers with wives so that colonization of the settlement can continue. You women will be an important part of that which is needed to insure the success of an English colony in America. Those who come to Virginia have dreams of a new land and a new order where all men, regardless of birth, have a chance to become landholders and live like gentlemen.

"How about women, sir, are they too allowed dreams of a new order?" Katherine asked.

"If it comes for men, lass, you can bet that women will be there with both hands out for their share," Captain Jamison answered with a twinkle in his eye.

"Every woman aboard this ship," he continued, "will have to accept a man from among those willing to pay her passage. Single yeoman and the likes will be waiting when we arrive. By the time we get to Jamestowne, everyone in the colony will know of our coming. They keep a close eye on the ships that come into the river because they are ever fearful that the Spanish may move on up from the South with the intentions of increasing

24

their claim. Life is hard in the colony, and every man needs a wife to share the work as well as to share his bed. Most of the men are good men, hard-working and with an eye to the future. At the beginning there were many stragglers but hard winters and starvation have thinned them out. With the increased market in tobacco, simple men now have the opportunity to become rich, and ownership of land is given to all."

"What choices are there, should any woman choose not to marry?" Katherine asked. "They may work five years as an indentured servant, if they can find someone willing to take them on and pay their passage. I feel they would be sorely used in that situation. The men there are a lusty lot and the women indentured to them are at their mercy. The wives of such men often feel threatened by a fresh young maiden and add their own kind of misery."

"I didn't come on this voyage to end up a servant," said Doris, one of the ladies of questionable character. "I mean to have me a land'older, I do."

"Yeah," the rest agreed.

At night in the darkness of their quarters the women sometimes talked and giggled until the hour was late. On one night during a lull, Charlotte was heard to ask Katherine if it was true that some women enjoyed being ravished by men.

Katherine, at a loss for answers, stayed quiet and Doris spoke up. "Lass, I believe ye have just moved beyond the expertise of the Lady Katherine. Fine ladies don't learn about sich in books. 'Tis meself who has the expertise when it comes to the ravishes of men and wot's enjoyable to whom. Most commonly ye git a man who satisfies his lust in ye and lets it go at that. 'Tis jest a few minutes of something ye learn to put up with fer a few pence. But now let me tell ye about that uncommon man 'at sometimes comes along. 'Tis a man what knows a woman and how to go about setten fire to 'er senses; once ye been ravished by such a man, ye'll never get enough."

"Wot does he do to ye 'at the common man don't do?" someone asked.

25

"Well first off, 'ee treats ye like yer something special. Rubbing yer body and enjoying the differences between a man and a woman." Seeing that she had the attention of everyone, Doris went on with an embarrassing description of foreplay. By the time she had finished, every woman in the group, including Katherine, had felt her body respond to the pictures Doris painted with her words.

"And have ye found such an uncommon man among the ship's crew? If so, would ye point 'em out to us?" Faye asked, breaking the tension and getting laughs.

After that night Doris became the teacher of night classes, and most of the women learned more than they wanted to know about men; their likes, their dislikes, and their anatomy.

Chapter 4

The day after Katherine left, Roberta had posted a letter to Jenny to apologize for sending Katherine unannounced and to further explain the situation. She knew that Katherine would give Jenny the bare details, if that. She asked that Katherine be allowed to stay there until she came of age and could receive her inheritance, or until other arrangements could be made. If her stay became inconvenient for Jenny or if Mr. Barlow found out Katherine's whereabouts, Roberta hoped they would have some alternative by then.

It was almost two weeks before a letter came by messenger from Jenny. In the letter she said that Katherine had never arrived and that she feared Katherine had been kidnaped. The abduction of maidens had recently become a common occurrence from the port at Plymouth. Wives were needed so badly in the new colony of Virginia that the men there were willing to trade 150 pounds of best leaf tobacco for their transportation, upon marriage. The companies backing the colony encouraged the shipment of women in an effort to prevent the failure of their colony and the loss of their investment. Tobacco was becoming a valuable import and women a lucrative export. In making inquiries of the driver of the coach from Aldershot, Jenny found that he remembered a lady who had been traveling alone; he thought she had accepted a ride from the Baleys. Although the Baleys denied any knowledge of Katherine, it was rumored that they had been connected with the abduction of other maidens through their tavern in Plymouth, and local authorities were investigating the situation. Jenny was awaiting word from further inquiries but held little hope. Three ships had sailed within a few days of Katherine's disappearance: the Marmaduke, the Warwick, and the Tyger. That was all the information Jenny had been able to obtain so far; if anything significant was forthcoming she would speed it to them.

27

Mr. Barlow had been in a rage since his return to find Katherine gone. Although the servants had claimed no knowledge of her disappearance, Roberta knew that she and Arthur were under suspicion. Now with this letter from Jenny, Roberta was at her wits' end as to what she should or could do to help find Katherine. It was more than she could do to carry on and appear ignorant of the whole affair when her entire being feared desperately for Katherine. In the kitchen, the morning after the letter had arrived, Roberta chanced to hear some servant's gossip concerning Carlton Edwards. He was a young man who had been a close friend of Katherine's brother Sam, before Sam's death in the duel five years earlier. Carlton had spent a great deal of time at the Arlington home, and Katherine, being younger than the boys, had adored Carlton with a fervor close to worship. Now it seemed that Carlton, having recently inherited his father's estate, found himself in danger of losing it all to his father's debtors. A plan began to form in Roberta's mind which involved her going to Mr. Barlow, and she knew that if the truth of her part in Katherine's disappearance came out, the punishment would be dismissal. Too much time had already passed and fear for Katherine would not allow Roberta to await solutions that might be less risky to herself. She wished she could go to Lady Marie, but that would be futile. With a slight straying from the truth, which Roberta knew would be forgiven by Katherine, she spoke to Mr. Barlow in his study that afternoon.

"Sire," she began, "I received a letter from Jenny Lawrence, a niece of Katherine's mother who lives in Plymouth. She writes that Katherine sent her word that she was coming there to stay with her, but she never showed up. Mrs. Lawrence fears that Katherine has been abducted and taken on a ship to the colonies." Roberta then read him all that Jenny had said about her inquires. "Sire, if I might make a suggestion."

Mr. Barlow, his rage now spent, was at a loss as to what he should tell the Blands and how to salvage something for himself from this disaster. "Well, go on, wench, what is it you wish to say?"

"Sire, I know ye tried to allow Katherine a choice in the matter of whom she would marry, but the gentlemen that were approved by you were not the kind that would appeal to a woman who has been raised with education and freedom of choice. I know that Master Arlington and Katherine's grandfather Randolph both indulged her wrongly, but never the less, wot's done is done. It come to me that if a certain gentleman, by the name of Carlton Edwards, could be persuaded to go and fetch Katherine from the colonies, your problems with Katherine might be solved. The gentleman I mention has recently inherited his family estate, only to find his father's gaming notes have put the estate into great debt. Katherine was at one time quite smitten by this gentleman, he being a close friend of young Samuel and often about the place."

"Leave the letter and let me find out what I can about this Edwards. I fear Katherine has lost her maidenhood by now, along with any chance of marriage to Mr. Bland."

"Jenny writes as if she believes me to know of Katherine's plans but ye know yeself how headstrong the girl can be."

"Aye, that I do. This Edwards, where might he be contacted?" Mr. Barlow asked as Roberta turned to go.

He has a house on Canon Row where he resides when in London, sire. 'Tis said he is there trying to buy time with promises of a prosperous harvest on their estate in Kent."

Carlton Edwards leaned back and stretched, having been bent for hours over a ledger in his study. From the window he could look out across the gardens which he had taken for granted all his life. Carlton was heartsick over the facts in the ledger; he had gone over them again and again, but there was no way to cover his father's notes without selling this property or their estate in Kent. The only practical thing to do was sell the house on Canon Row. The estate in Kent was his only means of supporting his mother and himself. The sale of the Canon Row property would not cover the notes entirely. He had been offered a good sum for the place, and with his mother's jewelry, some of the Kent horses, and his own carriage, he thought he could bargain for the notes. Most of the holders of the notes had been willing to work with him and give him a reasonable amount of time. Carlton could see no way in the future to pay the huge amount of debts, as they accumulated interest every quarter. His only hope lay in using cash from this house to get the largest notes discounted and paid as soon as possible.

The ringing of the bell at the street door caught Carlton's attention. He heard Sarah open the door and waited for her to announce yet another debtor. Instead she brought a message.

"I have a proposition that would be to our mutual benefit," the note read. "Could you meet with me this afternoon at two?" The note then gave the address of the Arlington house on White Hall Road. It was signed by Thomas Barlow.

Carlton knew of Mr. Barlow but could think of no reason why the man would wish to offer him a beneficial proposition. He hadn't seen any of the Arlington family since Sam's father had been killed in that accident about two years ago. He had heard that Katherine had grown into a real beauty but that her stepfather would not allow any man in to see her until a portion of her inheritance was assigned to him. More out of curiosity than hope, Carlton decided to hear what the man had to say.

When Roberta opened the door to Carlton, he thought her unusually pleased to see him. Little had changed in the house, which had been like a second home for him only a few years before. Everything here reminded him of Sam, and he felt the emptiness left by his best friend; nay, Sam was more like his brother.

"'Tis good to see ye lad," Roberta said as she led him to the study. "Much has changed in this house since ye came here with Sam. I pray that I have put my faith in the right person, for 'tis me who suggested your name to Mr. Barlow. I hope you will help us to find our beloved Katherine, and after finding her I pray ye take her from the clutches of her greedy stepfather."

With that Roberta knocked on the closed door of the study and walked away, leaving Carlton to enter at Mr. Barlow's request.

Carlton took the obvious seat across from Mr. Barlow's desk and waited as he put away the papers he had been working on. It was easy to see why Sam's mother had been foolishly taken by the man at the desk. Of even feature and good stature, Thomas Barlow would be considered a handsome man by most women. A sprinkling of gray at the temples was the only sign of age upon his body.

"I will get right to the point, Mr. Edwards," he said. "I have been told that at one time my stepdaughter Katherine was quite taken with you."

"That was but a childish infatuation. If the Lady Katherine has become the great beauty and quick wit for which she is reputed, then 'tis certain she has outgrown such infatuations."

"Ah, but you underestimate the romanticism of first love in the mind of a maiden. Having met you, a man of fine countenance, I can see that I have underestimated the importance of a handsome face. After making some inquires, I find yourself to be in circumstances similar to my own. It seems we both have a tendency to live above our means."

"If you mean the gambling debts, sir, 'tis true I have often been deceived by the Lady Luck. But 'twas my father who courted her to ruin before he died."

"I have a proposition to offer you that would help you recover what the Lady Luck has taken from you."

"And what do you propose, sir, that would be of such vast benefit that you would be willing to give it away to a stranger?"

"First of all, Mr. Edwards, I must explain to you the manner in which Katherine's inheritance is set up. As I find myself in a somewhat desperate situation, I will be honest with you. I have not been completely honest to the other gentlemen with whom I have bargained for a share of Katherine's inheritance. In order to get them to sign my agreements, I have insinuated that Katherine's inheritance was much less than the actual amount. Her father, Matthew Arlington, was a very rich man and either

31

very wise or with highly competent counsel. After the death of his son Samuel, Mr. Arlington revised his will in a way that leads me to believe he felt his heir and nephew Robert Arlington was somehow at fault for the death of his son. My wife, Marie, mentioned that he had become suspicious of Robbie before his death. Without a male heir there is no question as to Robbie's claim on all the Arlington estates, and mind you Matthew Arlington added much to them during his life time, for they were in a state of disrepair and with little money in the till when he inherited them. Unfortunately for myself, but fortunate for Katherine, he had great faith in her, more so than in his wife. A small portion, but an adequate amount counting interest, was put into an account to keep up the Arlington estates. Robbie will have a devil of a time using it for anything else. The remainder of Mr. Arlington's money was put into a trust for Katherine, the interest-- a good amount mind you-- to be used for the household and personal needs of his wife and daughter. That, Mr. Edwards, is all I have received from my wife's money with the exception of that brought in by the shipping firm. The Randolph shipping firm, in an unusual stipulation of Katherine's grandfather, stays with Katherine and then with her first son. Evidently, since she was an educated young lady, loved the business and loved the sea, her grandfather wanted it to stay in his own family after Sam's death. The business is prosperous, but as I have expensive tastes and control of the firm at this time, I have dipped heavily into the capital. Should Katherine have become married after the age of eighteen, the money in the trust and the shipping firm would be under the control of her husband. Though technically her grandfather left it so that Katherine has final say on anything to do with the shipping firm even in marriage. The gentlemen I have dealt with so far have had money of their own, and 'twas Katherine, who was of prime importance to them. The last, Harvey Bland, was extremely wealthy but a fool. Katherine refused to marry him and when I insisted, she ran away. My bargain with the others was that Katherine's money would all be put into the shipping firm, where I was to remain a full partner for ten years with a generous salary. Mr Arlington had requested that his barrister not reveal the amount to any man before the marriage, so as to protect Katherine from fortune seekers. This worked to my advantage in convincing the men that her dowry was adequate but not a great amount. As your circumstances are similar to my own, and I find myself in danger of losing everything, I have come up with what I consider a more than generous offer. To date, Katherine has rejected all the gentlemen suitors, so you remain the only man in whom she has ever shown an interest. It is up to you to go to her and fan the coals until there is a flame again. With the experience of which you are reputed and Katherine's great beauty to inspire you, this should be a simple matter."

"What's to keep me from accomplishing this without entering into any agreements with you?" Carlton asked.

"Because I know you will never find her without help from me. If you will agree to place one half of the trust into the shipping firm and make me a salaried partner, you will still have a small fortune. Enough, I guarantee, to more than cover your current debts, plus an ongoing salary from the firm. Time is running out for both of us. If Katherine should marry or die, there will be nothing for either of us. Right now the chances for marriage or death are higher than we want to believe."

"Are you saying that Katherine's life is in danger? I am afraid I do not understand, Mr. Barlow."

"A full explanation will be forthcoming, once the agreements are signed. 'Tis of the utmost urgency that we do this today."

I would like to read the agreements before I give you an answer." Carlton said.

Mr. Barlow produced two papers from his desk and stood looking out the window while Carlton read the contents.

"You, sir, are a scoundrel. There is enough money here to make us both rich. I would be happy to accept half, but there are two conditions. First, I will enter into marriage only with the consent of Katherine, for I do not intend to spend my life with a woman who hates me. Second, I must ask for a partnership

33

agreement which protects us both from such as has happened before to the shipping funds. An agreement which makes it impossible for either of us to take money from the account without the signature of the other. I would need a statement releasing the firm from any prior debts and any personal debts we may incur. This I consider a protection for each of us."

"Ah, I see my partner thinks very much like myself. Here is a standard partnership agreement. See that it satisfies your fears as to the firm's account. Other than taking on another whimpering widow, this is my last chance to make good. I intend to do everything I can to help make a success of the shipping firm. When you buy me out in ten years, I expect us both to be rich. You see, when I was robbing the firm of its capital, the potential for shipping profits was not as great as it has become recently. Increased interest in tobacco from America has changed everything."

"Now that the agreements are signed, please explain why Katherine's life may be in danger. She is the sister of a man I loved like a brother and I feel an obligation to see her safe."

"It was not all greed that made me promise the girl to Harvey Bland. Though foolishly in love with her and not of a fair countenance, the man was of such a temperament as to put up with Katherine's high-minded ways and of fortune enough to give back to Matthew Arlington some of what was taken from him. You see, I have through his papers and family grown to respect Mr. Arlington."

At a sign of impatience from Carlton, Mr. Barlow got back to his question. "Katherine, in an effort to get to a cousin in Plymouth, was abducted on arrival and put on a ship to Virginia. This has become a common practice, as men in the colonies are willing to pay for wives. According to my inquires, she is most likely on the Marmaduke, which left Plymouth two weeks ago. 'Twill be your job to go and fetch her. I can get you on a ship the day after tomorrow. Fortunate winds will get you there within a few weeks of the Marmaduke, for it is old and heavy with cargo. 'Tis a distressing fact that many who set out do not survive the trip. On Katherine's side is the fact that she sailed often to France, visiting her grandfather and attending school there. 'Tis my guess that her strong will alone could get her there. What worries me most is the damage that could befall her between here and there. Also, I have heard that the marriages take place within a day or two after arrival because lodging is scarce in the colony."

Chapter 5

October arrived with a nip of coolness in the air. It was daybreak on the last day of that month when the ship's passengers awoke to shouts of, "Land Ho." The women rushed to the rails to see only an irregular pattern of shadows skimming the horizon. By afternoon the brilliant foliage of the Chesapeake Capes became apparent, and excitement quickened the heart of every woman. Early evening brought them past a point of land on their left called Cape Henry and one to their right called Cape Charles. At dusk they entered the James River and dropped anchor within a quiet little harbor that was protected from the swell of the outer bay by a jutting point of land called Point Comfort. With Captain Jamison leading, they bowed their heads to thank the merciful God who had blessed them with a safe and speedy journey. Captain Jamison, in an effort to calm the women, told them it could take as much as two days to reach the wharfs of Jamestowne. Traveling the forty miles upriver would be much slower than ocean travel. The captain knew not the condition of the river due to storms or droughts that may have affected the river since his last trip; thus, he preferred to start the trip up river in daylight.

The women slept in excited snatches through the night, like children on the night before Christmas. Katherine awoke to find the ship making its way up the James, and she hurried above board to see this new land she had read and heard so much about. From the rail she could see the large trees that had been growing, untouched, for generations. Their luxuriant foliage was ablaze with the brightest of nature's palette. The far-reaching expanse of hill and valley lay unbroken by road or path and all along the river there was an atmosphere of mystery and solitude. As Katherine stood looking out at what others had called the Eden of the world, she could identify with their feelings. Looking down into the water of the James River she saw again the beauty of the river's banks as they were reflected there. She also saw a reflection of herself in the water below and even though she looked the same, she knew she was not the naive young woman who had begun this journey. The long weeks aboard ship in such intimate living conditions with the others had made her realize how sheltered her own life had been. She had gained an education that money could never have bought. Through the particulars of the lives of the women who traveled with her she had learned about lack, physical and emotional lack. From their experiences she had learned of men and men's desires. Nothing had prepared her for the revulsion she had felt upon learning of the lecherous and perverse desires of some men. Unprepared also was she to find that their descriptions of the natural desires of men could excite desire within her own body. The limited lives and thinking expressed by some of the women had made Katherine aware of the prisons we allow to be built around us, by others, by circumstance, by ignorance, and by erroneous beliefs. Lost in her thoughts, Katherine had not noticed that Bertha, one of the women who had kept to herself throughout the trip, stood beside her at the rail. When she saw that Katherine had noticed her, she moved closer.

"'Tis curious, I am, to know what ye be thinking so 'ard on, Miss Katherine."

"I saw my reflection in the water Bertha, and I was thinking that even though I look the same, I am not the same person who began this trip. I have gained so much from the time spent with all of you. There is so much in life that I would never have known or understood, had I not been brought aboard. We are not so different, you know? Circumstances have made us appear to be different, but I can see now that we are not."

"'Tis like me John, ye sound. 'Tis John I go to marry in this new country. Ee thinks that in Virginia, 'twill be different from England. All men will have the same chance at a good life in America, says ee. If a man be of good mind and good back, says John, ee can be a land'older in jest a few years. I do 'ope we live to see 'at day. John, so got 'es 'eart set on it."

"I hope your John is right Bertha, and that he realizes his dreams. I believe that is the way God intended life to be. Perhaps the Lord will have his way in this new world."

The following morning, signs of the English colony could be seen on the banks of the river. At every wharf along the way tattered children and grown-ups ran to cheer them on. An English ship meant beer and foodstuff and news of home. The crude wharfs marked the river access for the plantations, or "hundreds," as they were called. So named for the 1250-acre parcels of land from which they began. Captain Jamison had sent a small boat ahead on the night they entered the river. The two men in it were to stop off in Jamestowne and spread the news of the women before going upstream to Montgomery's Hundred with the sealed envelope from Captain Jamison.

The women grew tired of standing at the rail and went below to make preparations for their landing in Jamestowne. Captain Jamison had said they should reach Jamestown by the following morn, at which time the women, except Katherine, would have three days to choose the man who would pay their fare. As for Katherine, there was no way to determine how Payton Montgomery would wish to handle that situation.

Word of the Marmaduke moving toward Jamestowne had already reached Payton Montgomery when the small boat arrived with the message from Captain Jamison. Payton felt only relief after reading the note. Perhaps now he could get the seed planted for an heir before it was too late. The colony guaranteed no man a tomorrow. The fevers, the Indians, and starvation were as wolves, ever lurking near, ever taking their toll. Better men than himself were taken in a blink of the eye. As he considered Captain Jamison's message again he wondered if perhaps he should have waited until time allowed him to go and pick a wife for himself. There were certain qualities that he would wish to be present in a woman who was mother to his heir. Also he had little patience for a woman who could not cope with the hardships of life on the 'hundred.' In fact Payton would rather have had a good sturdy common woman for a wife in this place, but he owed it to his heir to give him as much influence as possible. He knew the importance of name and breeding in dealing with the Crown. In the governing of the colony it was only men such as himself, with breeding and education, who could communicate with the representatives of the Crown and the merchants who financed the colony. Until the common men could see themselves as equals, they would not be seen as equal. Until they could gain the education and confidence needed to deal with men whose only interest was in profits, the governing process would be left to men of like mind--some of whom were not always inclined to consider the best interests of the common man. Payton had quickly become aware that more than one generation would pass before a new order could take root in Virginia. If men with determination did not see it through and produce heirs to carry on their work, Virginia would turn into another England. Payton thought of dear friends, wasted away from starvation or disease, the dream of equality alive on their dying breath. Too many had given too much to let that dream slip away, now or in the future. As Payton made ready his household for the coming of a wife, word spread quickly and he sensed the excitement and concern of the people of Montgomery's Hundred. Again he could only hope that the lady was up to the challenges of this land, and that she would not be a disappointment or burden to the people of his plantation as they rejoiced in her coming.

Payton was up with the crowing of the cock. In meticulous attire he soon had his chaise hitched and ready to go. As he suspected, everyone on the 'hundred' was alert, taking note of this occasion as if it were a fairy tale to tell again and again in the drudgery of everyday life. Potter Ben opened the gate for him and waved him through.

"Oh, well," Payton told himself as he pushed aside his doubts and began the four hour trip to Jamestowne, "there is something to be said for the convenience of a man being able to release his natural urges in the comfort of his own home without the worry of filth and disease. Perhaps too, a wife will put to rest the flirtations of other men's wives, which seem to forever be putting me at odds with men I respect and admire." With that thought came a pain long ago imbedded in his heart, and he felt a deep sorrow for his father. By now his father would be aware that the young wife he had taken after his mother's death was no more than a harlot. Payton felt sure that Sara's passion for men had not cooled when his father banished him from the home. Payton had never given Sara the slightest encouragement. He had, in fact, become so good at avoiding the wench, she had grown hostile, and, having the ear of his father, had led him to believe Payton was making the advances. Payton often wondered if Sara had then turned her lust to his older brother Paul and how his father had reacted to that. Although married and his wife with child when Payton left, Paul was not above accepting Sara's favors unless he resented the fact that they had been offered to Payton first. His father cared deeply for the comely young wench; Payton could understand this and forgive his father's harsh words and actions. It had been harder to forgive Paul. He had seen the obvious traps that Sara laid for Payton and had not said a word on Payton's behalf when his father asked him to leave.

The cool morning had warmed with the sun and Payton, following the river road, stopped to let the horses drink from a cleared spot where the river came near the dusty road. When winter came the road would likely become impassable. The timing of Captain Jamison in bringing a wife was probably as good as there was. At least she would have a couple of months to recover from the trip before winter became really harsh. The storehouses at the 'hundred' were full from an abundant harvest. His tobacco yield had been the highest he had produced so far. The big amber leaves now hung from the poles in their sheds, cured and ready for shipment on the Marmaduke. The other men at the hundred had also done well with their tobacco crops. He suspected that one or two would be off on their own before long. He only hoped they could finish burning off the new

40

ground for next year's crop before any of the men left. He had to wait for rain before he could do any more burning.

Again Payton wondered about the woman who waited for him in Jamestowne. He could not imagine any circumstance that would put a desirable lady on a ship to Virginia. He knew that the one who waited for him had none of the qualities that would attract a man of power, land, or money; otherwise her father would not have allowed her to leave. Of course, he had known fine ladies that one had to look deep to see the beauty within them, women whose fathers had paid dearly to see them wed.

With guilt, Payton thought about Jamie and prayed a silent prayer that the new wife would have some time to give to the child. Witless though the boy seemed, Payton knew he needed love and attention. Such a bright child he had been before the shock of seeing his mother and little sister killed by the Indians. If only Payton had been home that day, perhaps he could have prevented their deaths. Payton hardly knew how to explain Jamie and his condition to this Lady Katherine. Seems the lad would have recovered from the shock by now. Perhaps he would have if Payton had taken time at the beginning to work with him, but Payton's own grief was so consuming that he had hardly been able to get up and put forth the effort to make it through the day. Payton had loved the boy as much as it was possible to love another man's child, but there was no way to describe the depth of the love he had for the daughter born of Angie and himself. In Priscilla he had caught glimpses of the very best of himself, of Angie, and of his beloved mother, for whom the child had been named. Nary an evening passed that he didn't miss her delight in his return from field or woods. In his better moments he thanked God for the gift of knowing such love, however short their time together. In his worst moments he cursed a God that would let an innocent child suffer such brutality. Payton wiped away a tear and saw that he was within a few miles of Jamestowne. Ahead he could see small groups of people walking toward the town to greet the ship that by now had probably reached the wharfs. Before approaching the friends and neighbors who walked up ahead, he needed to put aside thoughts of the past and return to the present. He had hashed and rehashed all this, he knew it was futile to look back. He prayed a quick prayer that this woman would be acceptable, at least enough for a peaceful existence together. That being his highest expectation, the most he hoped to get for his money, besides an heir of course, he flicked the reins and caught up with the others.

The girls had found it hard to sleep as the ship made the final knots up river by moonlight. Daybreak found them preparing themselves as best they could for the men who would be waiting. Katherine chose a straight-bodied gown of green silk and arranged her hair simply in an upward sweep. They had aired out their clothes the day before and the dampness of the air had removed some of the wrinkles. Katherine had shared her scented soap and had tried to help them with the curling and crimping of their hair. Now as each surveyed the results in Katherine's hand mirror, she gave them words of encouragement and tried to soothe their rattled nerves. Charlotte, having been in Doris's paints and toilet water, looked like a clown and smelled too strongly of jasmine.. In exasperation Katherine insisted on helping her tone it down a bit, then let her go with a hug and an assurance that her offer of help still stood. By now Charlotte had gotten caught up in the excitement of landholders and chamber pots made of gold.

The roar of a crowd distracted them from their primping. Above board they moved to the rail to find they had reached the loading wharfs of Jamestowne and a crowd of shabby spectators lined the shore. Rising above the wharfs on a peninsula, a jumble of rough wooden buildings spread to the right of an older palisade, which enclosed the oldest part of the town. Katherine was reminded of the colonies in Ireland that she had sailed to before her father's death, and with a heartsick feeling she longed for home, home as it had been then. Men with dirty hair and rotten teeth called out crude phrases to the women aboard ship, and Katherine felt a real concern for the girls who had become her friends. Doris yelled back at the men and then assured the girls that a little soap and water could clean some of them up nicely.

When the planks were in place to unload, the girls moved shyly toward the crowd of men. A small group of women stepped forth to greet the girls; to Katherine's relief they looked much like the women one would find in any English village. One nice-looking, grey-haired woman who seemed to be the leader, announced to the crowd that a midday meal would be spread in the church-yard, and all were invited to attend. The women embraced the maidens and led them up the hill toward the church. As Katherine watched them go she felt alone and fearful of the future. Going below deck, she packed her things back into the trunks. She wondered if this was a sign that deep down she had already accepted the man who was on his way to retrieve her. It had always been her belief that she would know the man who was right for her the minute she met him. It was hard to put into words that quality she looked for in a man. She could only describe him as a man secure within himself, having developed a respect for self that came through the realization of his own potential. Such men seemed to be more aware of the potential in others, assuming a common respect for all humanity. She guessed you could call it a confidence in themselves that extended itself out to a confidence in others. This had been a special quality of her father and her grandfather, a rare quality that one recognized even when one could hardly describe it. Taking a book of poetry, Katherine went above board to wait; she knew that in the end she would not compromise herself even though threatened by fearful alternatives.

Chapter 6

It was near midday and the crowds had grown. They stood around in groups visiting while awaiting the coming meal and another look at the maidens. A stir among the crowd attracted Katherine's attention and brought her to the rail to see a chaise drawn by two fine horses making its way down the hill. It slowly parted the crowd, several of the men taking a place beside it and following along until it came to a stop. Others gathered around extending their hand in greeting and blocking her view of the man driving. Some of the men seemed to be. in a conversation with the driver; others admired the chaise and patted the flanks of the horses. After a few minutes he, and the group that surrounded him, made their way to the planks that formed a ramp for the ship.

The man who stepped forth to board the ship wore a broadleafed hat of Flemish beaver, a splendid feather curled rakishly over a leather hatband. Nodding his head at men along the wharf, the man moved with swift assurance up the ramp. He paused only long enough to allow a hogshead of beer to be rolled in front of him, then headed toward the captain's quarters. From where Katherine stood she could see him plainly. A knee-length clock was thrown back gracefully over one shoulder exposing a leather doublet slashed liberally to show fine, full linen shirt sleeves. Knee-breeches, edged with points of gold, met the tops of high boots, these made of Spanish leather and turned over into cuffs. Although his attire was slightly outdated, there was nothing ostentatious about it. Here was a man who dressed to please himself and to show his station in life. His manner and confidence were such that one could not help being impressed. Katherine, having been served a steady diet of superficial dandies, was more than impressed. It was if this man fit some ideal that had lain hidden within the inner recesses of her mind until just this moment, and now she found herself afraid to hope that this man was Payton Montgomery. Even more afraid was she that he was not, for then she would have to take another. As he neared the captain's door, Katherine could see his hair from the back; unpowdered, dark brown, and curling in great loose rings. Before knocking, he removed gloves that were gauntleted and fringed; he tucked them into a rich sword-belt. What appeared to be a genuine Andrea Ferrara sword, encased in silver, picked up sun rays and flashed patterns of light on the door as it opened. He took the captain's outstretched hand and grasped the captain's shoulder with his other hand. They stood thus for a minute or two, heads bowed in conversation. The captain then showed him in and shut the door.

Alone on the deck except for the members of the crew who were rolling hogsheads down the ramp, Katherine turned back to the rail to watch the crowds. At the sound of footsteps near her she turned to see Captain Jamison coming toward her; he took her elbow to lead her to his quarters. The man stood with his back to them as they entered through the open door. He studied a map on the wall behind the captain's desk, but turned at the sound of their entrance. This was the very same man that Katherine had observed from the rail. He removed his hat and swept into a polite bow. A weakness moved through Katherine and settled in her knees as she tried to appear unmoved. Silently he looked her up and down. His expression was one of stifled amusement when he spoke. "Miss Lawrence, my name is Payton Montgomery. A year or so ago, I put out word among the ship's captains who travel here that I would like a wife. A woman of some breeding that would not shame my heirs. After spreading the word, I began to wonder about the woman who would be brought to me. In all my imagining, I never imagined that I would be forced to turn down a woman because she was too beautiful and too well bred for this struggling colony. On my 'hundred,' there is a rule; every hand that partakes of food must give back its equal or better in work. I cannot be the first to break my own rule, nor do I have the means or the time to coddle a woman such as yourself." He then turned to the captain.

45

"Captain Jamison, I appreciate what you have tried to do for me. I must say I am taken aback. I never expected so fine a woman on this side of the ocean."

"Sire, they's a lot more to this lass than meets the eye," the captain answered. Seeing himself about to be the loser, he went on. "This woman, by mixing her fruit preserves and water, has stolen at least two or three of the women aboard from the devil hisself. Took me ship right out from under me, she did. Had me crew and all me rigging utilized for a massive clothes washing. The whole of Englynd is laughing right now about the Marmaduke sailing with women's underwear flapping from the mizzen ratlines. Sire, I beg ye not to make any hasty judgments about this lady. Ye don't have to take the word of the one to gain. Walk out there and ask any one of me crew which woman out of the eleven that sailed got the most backbone, they will tell ye the same."

By this time Katherine was beginning to feel like a rejected sack of wool. "Mr. Montgomery, if you find me a disappointment, then concern yourself no further with my welfare. No one has yet asked me if I would be willing to stay in this uncivilized country."

"I apologize, Miss. It may be that I have misjudged you. I only meant to save myself another grave to dig." A sadness had appeared for a second in his eyes and then it was gone.

"Yes, Sire, ye do misjudge," Captain Jamison said. "This maiden, a lady by all standards, has shown an unbelievable resilience in making the trip. Fared as well as the best of us, she did. She is uncommonly educated and has during this trip taught the other girls to read and write. I know you will find her an asset to your life and your purpose here. I must warn you, however, that she does have a mind of her own and is hard to turn once 'tis set." Captain Jamison winked.

Payton Montgomery turned to Katherine with a smile. It was as if every feature in his face conspired to win her heart, even though he wanted her not. An unfamiliar excitement stirred and her heart was drawn to him as if reunited to some missing part of its very self. His deeply tanned face intensified the blue of his eyes and made radiant a smile of even white teeth. The scent of him, carried to her as he turned, was that of leather and a man of clean habit. As he took her hand into his work-hardened hand, she looked deeply into clear blue eyes fringed by black lashes and though she could not see past them to his thoughts, her heart sensed him to be a man of good report.

"Lady Katherine, I am overwhelmed by your comeliness. My mind was prepared for the worst and has not yet adjusted to this turn of events. I don't mean to look a gift horse in the mouth, but what circumstances would put a lady such as yourself on the block for a pittance in tobacco when a wise father in England could swap you off for titled estates?"

"My father has been dead these past three years, Sire. My mother remarried, allowing my stepfather to take over. In an effort to escape that situation, I find myself here."

"I see, and what do you expect here? In England a woman such as yourself would be courted and given time to plan an elaborate wedding. She would then live a life filled with social engagements and merriment. I can offer you none of that. My plan was to take you to my plantation today, have the woman who works for me there to protect your reputation, and then marry on the morrow. The people of my plantation are free families who work hard to survive and find little to celebrate. I hoped that we could marry there with some small amount of celebration, as they are ever hungry for anything that appeals to their romantic notions of home."

"I expect, Sire, that we shall proceed with your plan, given your word of honor that should I choose not to go through with this wedding, you will see that I am returned to the ship and Captain Jamison paid in full for my fare."

"You are asking me to risk funds that are especially dear to me at this time, and that on a woman's indecisive nature?"

"I can assure you that I am not an indecisive woman, once I have the information to make a decision. It is to your benefit in the long run, as well as my own that I arrive at this decision with

47

my eyes open. I will return to England only if I find what you offer more unbearable than what faces me in England. I do not ask you to risk your funds lightly. At this time I find no fault with your person, but I can see that life here would require an enormous amount of fortitude, perhaps more than I have to give."

"'Tis a rare woman that can be completely honest, especially to herself. I am also impressed with your astuteness concerning life here. Lady Katherine, we will see if you are worth the risk. Captain Jamison will bear witness that I have heard your terms and agreed to them."

"In that case I am more than ready to set foot on land. My trunks are packed and waiting."

Captain Jamison called two men forth to put her trunks on the chaise. Walking beside Payton and Katherine, he wished them well and told Payton they would see to the loading of his tobacco on the day after tomorrow. With a gentle hand on her arm, Payton led her down the ramp. Waving and acknowledging the remarks of those who had waited out of curiosity, he spoke to Katherine in a low voice, "At least my creditors will be heartened to think that maybe you come with a dowry."

Looking up at him, Katherine was taken aback by the smile that he was giving the audience. She was enchanted with this man. Everything about this unusual arrangement felt right.

As the trunks were being strapped on the chaise, Katherine heard the bell being tolled for the meal at church. "If it pleases you, Sire, I would like to take part in the midday meal before we go. I am starved for something besides salt pork and I would like to say good-bye to my friends from aboard ship. Perhaps too, I should meet the people of the colony; that might have some bearing on my final decision."

"I was just about to make the same suggestion, Lady Katherine. I too am hungry and in need of speaking with some members of council who will likely be among the crowd. My horses need a short rest before setting out again with this extra weight. Let's take the chaise to the livery stable, that they may attend them. We can walk to the church from there, and you can get your land legs back."

Katherine admired Payton's fine form as he gave orders to the man at the stable to feed and water his team. With horses settled, Payton took her arm and they began their walk up the hill to the church. Katherine felt a quickening of her heartbeat at his gentle touch and a comfort in being at his side.

"I know you must find Jamestowne crude and uncivilized. I'm sorry to say that you won't find it much better at Montgomery's Hundred. Cleaner and smaller, but of the same rough wood. I do have a comfortable home and people who will treat you well. Our plantation is nearly four years old and has become more self-sufficient than most on the river. Only those who came here before the starving time, or before our discovery of tobacco as a profitable crop, can appreciate how far the colony has come. This new world is a challenge, Lady Katherine, but it offers a new beginning to those willing to meet that challenge. Few of the men who own land here would have had that advantage in England. For most it is their one chance to make a better life for themselves and their families. It is to that end that we sacrifice the comforts and security of our homeland."

As they neared the crowd at the church, Katherine stood straight and walked with pride on the arm of a man who was immediately recognized and revered as a leader. Taking her toward two well-dressed gentlemen and an attractive gray-haired lady, Payton introduced her first to John Rolfe, he having returned to the colony after the death of his wife, Pocahontas, in England. Ralph and Elizabeth Hamor were the couple with Mr. Rolfe. Payton, John, and Ralph, all being members of the House of Burgesses, soon left her with Elizabeth and joined a group of men who were seated at a table in discussion. Elizabeth was the same lady that Katherine had noticed from the ship, taking charge of the women. As soon as Payton left her, Elizabeth began to question her as to her family in England. Katherine's experience with Mrs. Baley and her recent conversation with Payton helped her to end the inquiry quickly. "Elizabeth, I feel that this new world will demand that we let go of our past and concentrate on what we need to become in order to secure the future of the colony."

With a hearty laugh, Elizabeth apologized. "Thank you, my dear, for putting me in my place. Old habits die hard. What you say is more true than you could possibly know. I like you Lady Katherine. That doesn't mean that I or any woman in the colony will soon forgive you for being the one to get Payton Montgomery. I think we are all a little in love with him."

"Don't condemn me yet, for nothing is settled," Katherine returned jokingly. "Do you know where the girls from the ship are being kept? I don't see any of them."

"They should be just finishing up a little acquaintance reception in the church. We have allowed the single men to meet with them so that they might have a chance to get to know one another. By the end of this day they will most likely be paired up, then married in a group wedding tomorrow or the day after. We have neither the time nor the facilities for prolonged courtships in Jamestowne. I too found this shocking at first and thought it sad that necessity brought so many compromises, but then we have all heard it said that you never really know anyone until you have lived with them."

Chapter 7

Walking back to the stable, Payton explained that the House of Burgesses was the legislature, elected by the people of the colony to represent them with the Virginia Company in London who held the charter under which the Virginia colony had been seated. A few years ago, Governor George Yeardley, under instructions from the Company, had abolished the strict military regulations that had been in effect since the early days of the colony and had placed Virginia under the common law of England. According to a five-year plan put into effect by Sir Edwin Sandys and the general court of the Company in England, the colony would have more self-control, and anyone who came over would be allowed to own land. The amount of acreage depended upon how many they brought with them or a seven-year tenure. Governor Yeardley had at that time allowed the people of each plantation to elect their representatives. The House of Burgesses, along with an appointed council, had the power to pass local laws, subject of course to the veto of the Company. This assembly had been meeting since July of 1619. Payton, having bought land as a stockholder in the company before this five-year plan, was an appointed council member and an elected member of the House of Burgesses. Due to a lack of men with education and understanding of the political system, it was common for a few men to hold several positions in Virginia.

Having helped Katherine up into the chaise to begin the trip home, Payton gave Katherine a chance to look over the new land. He marveled again at his good fortune in bringing home such a woman. Had he gone and picked a woman for himself, he was not sure he would have done so well. Not only was she a pleasure to look upon, he found that to be in her company was also a pleasure. Her honesty and intelligence had immediately put him at ease. The questions she asked and her obvious interest in the colony gave rise to a feeling that her decision to stay or go would be fairly made. He sensed in her an inner strength that would prove useful should she stay. Of a serious nature, with a maturity beyond her years, she was not a woman with whom one had to play the games of flattery and courtship. In truth, he sensed that she would be insulted by such banal attempts. His respect for her grew moment by moment.

"Tell me the state of your relations with the Indians. Have they learned to accept the English settlers and begun to live peacefully with them?" Katherine asked, breaking the comfortable silence they had established.

"The marriage of John Rolfe to Pocahontas seemed to be the beginning of a tolerance toward the English, at least as long as her father, Powhatan, was alive. When he died, two years ago this past spring, his lame brother, Opitchapan, succeeded him and things stayed much the same as before. Now Opitchapan has turned the leadership over to their brother, Opechancanough, a man who has been in several conflicts with the Spanish to the south and sees all whites as intruders. I can understand his fear, for it is true that the Powhatans are being pushed farther and farther back. Tobacco is sensitive to blights and cannot be grown year after year on the same land. It requires the constant cultivation of new land. I fear for our safety under the leadership of Opechancanough and try to stress this to the colonists but they fall easily into complacency."

"Does that mean we will be in constant danger at all times?" she asked.

"Yes, and I would ask that you never forget it even for a moment. This seems like the time to tell you of my first wife and child. Angela was a very good friend who was raised on my father's estate in Northumberland. Circumstances which I won't go into forced her to come to me shortly after I arrived in Virginia. She was carrying the child of a man who had been killed in England, and she feared for her own safety as well as that of her unborn child. I, having just erected on my land an ill-protected hut, could not turn her away. The birth of her son was soon followed by the death of the woman who tended my home, so Angela and I became wed, that being the only acceptable way we could continue to live together. Our relationship remained — that of friends but she felt it her duty to satisfy my natural urges and she bore for me a daughter. Priscilla, named after my belated mother, became the love of my life. Of course I had grown to love Jamie as my own, but my beautiful little daughter touched my heart in a way that it had never been touched and she became more precious to me than anything in my life, perhaps more precious than God will allow. One morning I left early with three of my tenants to hunt meat for our table. We returned to find our homes burnt to the ground and most of our families dead. Jamie had crawled into a clay oven the women used for baking and from there he watched the brutal massacre. Since that day, more than two years ago, he has not said a word and appears to be struck dumb. My sorrow was so great that I could not help myself or the child. I fear the time to help him has passed. My guilt and my helplessness toward the child tend to make me avoid him. It is my wish that, should you decide to stay, you might take an interest in him and show him some affection for he was a good child with a good mind."

Tears had been streaming down Payton's cheeks as he told the story, and Katherine suspected that a deep wound had been reopened in the telling. He took a moment to regain his composure before going on.

"To be ever aware of what is going on around you is most important and to have clear in your mind the proper actions to take in case of attack. These will become known to you after you have become familiar with the plantation. The men who trade among the Indians of different tribes say the Powhatans are the most treacherous of the lot. It is their custom to become friendly and gain your trust before an attack. They rely heavily on surprise. A few will come bearing gifts of fish or fowl, while the others hide to await the appointed time. They have used this method effectively to destroy neighboring tribes and English families.

"What would be expected of me in a household such as yours?" she asked.

53

"One of the women, whose whole family was killed in the same massacre as Angie, has taken care of my house since I built it. She takes care of Jamie also. She suffers from a sort of chronic depression and often functions as in a trance, yet she takes adequate care of my home and the necessities of Jamic. You would be free to find the place most suited to your talents and apply them in the manner of your choice. I have no desire to turn this woman out or take away all of her duties, for I fear she may succumb to the depression and give up."

"Where would we be married? What kind of ceremony do you propose?"

"We have our own chapel and our own minister, Reverend Swann. I would hope that you have with you something suitable and fashionable to wear, for there will be no time or material to provide such as would be expected. 'Tis a certainty that all eyes will be upon you, taking note of the smallest detail. Should you decide to stay and be my wife, I would like you to know that I would be proud to walk down the aisle with you. I will do everything in my power to protect you and anything within reason to keep you content as long as we may live together."

"Katherine could feel the sincerity of his promise, but as of yet, she had no answer for him. She knew her heart had relented the moment she looked into his eyes, but with her life at stake she wasn't ready to trust her heart."

Before dusk Payton told her they were almost there. Katherine felt tired from the long ride and worn from the stress of all that had taken place. She smoothed her hair and fluffed her dress, then with shoulders straight and head held high she rode into Montgomery's Hundred. The entrance to the Hundred was like a little village enclosed in a palisade. Their arrival had been announced by the look-out, and curiosity had brought them all out to see her. Payton stopped before the small crowd and helped her down from the chaise.

"I would like you all to meet Lady Katherine Lawrence. She is here to make the decision whether to stay or not, so I ask you to be your most charming selves. We are both tired and wish to take a short rest before supper; at that time she will be happy to meet you all." Payton then handed the reins to a man who stood waiting. Katherine smiled to the crowd and waved a temporary good-bye before Payton took her arm to walk through to the back of the palisade, where his home sat inside a triangular fort, similar to that of Jamestowne but not as big. The house was a two-story of wood frame with a porch on the front and glazed windows. Its basic structure was much like the small house of England, a type often built to accommodate small city lots. The church had been the only other building she had noticed with windows. As Payton helped her up the steps, the door was opened to them by a drab woman with hair unkempt and sad-colored garments. Her facial expressions remained unchanged throughout the introduction.

"Hello, Molly," Katherine said, taking a hand that hung loosely at her side. "Should I stay here, I will have to depend heavily on you, for I know nothing about life on a plantation."

Although Katherine still noticed no change in her expression, Payton saw a small sigh of relief followed by a softening of her eyes. Both signs that Katherine had met with some small amount of approval and that Molly felt reassured that her position was secure for the time being. He was thankful that Katherine had handled it thus.

Following Payton through the hall that ran the middle of the house, she was surprised to find the house well furnished and seemingly quite comfortable. The front room to the right of the hall was a parlor where a small fire burned. It was decorated in such a fine manner it felt very much the same as an English parlor. Also on the right just past the parlor was a library. Katherine was delighted to see the familiar names of books she loved; those unknown to her piqued her interest. She had not expected such a collection on this side of the ocean. To the left of the hall there seemed to be only a great room with a huge fireplace, centered so that it served the dining area as well as the family living area, the whole of this room giving one a feeling of being in a country lodge. The hall ran to a back door where one stepped down into a kitchen. Attached to the kitchen were Molly's private quarters, which they did not enter. Before they left, Payton showed her the latch on the door that went outside from the kitchen, explaining that the rope which released a strong inside latch was put through a hole during the day and pulled back through at night to keep it locked from the outside. The front door was the same, and though Molly would see to this one, it was imperative that she in the event of his absence, remember the front door. The stairs which led up from the hall to the left of the front door were of black walnut and intricately carved, being in her estimation one of the most beautiful features of the house. Following Payton up she found a central hall there separating two bedrooms on one side from a large bedroom and bath chamber on the other side. Payton's room being the large one with heavy furniture of Spanish oak and bearing an atmosphere of masculinity. Walking to the front end of this room Katherine discovered a wonderful view of the James river. The other front bedroom, also with a river view, was the guest room and Katherine's trunks had been placed there without her having noticed them brought in. The door to the back bedroom was closed. Before entering, Payton knocked softly, explaining that this was Jamie's room and that it frightened him for the door to be opened without warning. Inside Katherine found a child's room with an accumulation of toys, books, and things of interest to a young man, all as untouched as the day they were bought. Propped up in a clean bed sat a frail child with fair golden curls and blank eyes. Katherine went straight to the child and embraced him. There was something hauntingly familiar about the boy and her heart knew an instant affinity for him.

"Hello, Jamie, my name is Katherine, and I have just come here from England on a ship. I wish you were able to talk to me and tell me about your plantation. Tomorrow morning I will come to your room and get you to go around the plantation with me." Seeing no response at all, she kissed his cheek and followed Payton out, parting in the hall to go to their separate rooms and rest for a bit before supper.

Katherine took from her trunk the white brocade with silver threads and hung it to allow the wrinkles to fall. She took also a maroon velvet, laying it out to put on before supper. After finding all that she would need to go with it, she took the lavender soap to the wash basin and found fresh water awaited her there. After striping down to her petticoats, she washed, then crawled between fine damask sheets, not to sleep but to relax her tense nerves and rest her weary back. The soft feather bed was a luxurious treat, one she would never again take for granted.

A table that ran most of the length of the long house in the compound had been set with some of the summer's harvest, along with meats and fish and fowl. A lower table had been set up for the children, and some of them had already taken their seats. When Payton entered with Katherine on his arm the people stood back with a kind of bashfulness and awe. After only a minute of silence, a comely little girl with a fine, thickset head of hair and rosy cheeks walked straight up to Katherine and took her hand.

"Yer posed to set right here," she said, leading Katherine to a place near the head of the table. "I can't set with you cause I'm too little." She skipped over to a place at the children's table, looking quite proud of herself, and everyone laughed. That seemed to break the tension and soon everyone was seated and involved in the food and their own conversations, while keeping an ear out for any snatch of news or interesting morsel they might overhear from the end of the table where Payton and Katherine sat. The men were anxious to know the news from England. Between mouthfuls they asked concerning the health of King James I and of the current state of affairs in Bohemia, where English volunteers had gone to support King James' son-in-law, Frederick V. Katherine told them of the Bohemian defeat at the Battle of the White Mountain near Prague and of the ban under which Frederick had been placed by the Holy Roman Empire. She told them that Francis Bacon had been pardoned by the king, the charges of corruption dropped. That John Williams had been made Lord Keeper and Lionel Cranfield was now Lord Treasurer.

"Sounds as if the king has put foxes in to guard the hen house," Payton replied to this last bit of news.

Katherine told them that the Fortune Theater in London had burned and asked them if they had heard that Oliver Cromwell was denounced last year for his participation in the "disreputable game of cricket." They talked about the twelve-year truce between Holland and Spain that was ending this year, and there were predictions that the war would resume between them.

At the close of the evening Payton had never been prouder of any woman than he was of Katherine. Walking back he could only offer a fervent prayer that she would decide to stay. "Surely God, you would not send so perfect a woman to me and then take her away."

"'Tis a refreshing change," he said to Katherine, "to find a lady who is not so self-absorbed, one who has some comprehension of the world. I am indeed pleased to know you and to have had you here. With that he took her in his arms and held her close for a moment, then tilting her chin up with one hand he gave her a gentle kiss on her lips. As she forced her weak legs to climb the steps, with his help, she knew that if she left this man she would be leaving the only man who could ever matter to her. Once in bed, she told herself that she would awake with a surety as to what to do. She considered for a while what it might be like living here and found the prospect not unthinkable. She thought too of the loneliness of the past five years of her life, with first Samuel, then Father leaving her. Her mother was not really there either, not since the death of Samuel. In truth she had more for which to stay here than she had in England.

There was the child Jamie, who desperately needed someone, and of course there was Payton, beside whom, all men would pale in her eyes from this day forth. There were the people of the plantation too. They had already made her feel as

58

if she belonged. At this moment she could not imagine herself going back to the loneliness of her past.

"Still, I have always been able to think more clearly in the morning light," she told herself. "And without the sweet nectar of Payton's kiss upon my lips."

Chapter 8

Katherine awoke early, refreshed and excited. It was a crispy cool morning, and she was anxious to get moving. There was one more thing she wanted to do before telling Payton of her decision. Dressing casually in what had been one of her mother's riding habits, she put on the Spanish leather boots, knotted her hair quickly, topped it with a felt riding hat, stuck a pin through to hold it in place, and was on her way into Jamie's room to get him up. Through the open door of Payton's room she could see he was already up and gone. The soft knock woke Jamie from his sleep, but he was not startled. Katherine entered and looking through a chest and on pegs, found clothes to get him dressed.

"Do you remember me, Jamie? I'm Katherine and I have come to take you with me to look over the plantation. Jump up and put on clothes; I can't take you out in night rails."

At first he just lay there as if she had not spoken at all.

"Jamie, you may have been rendered speechless, but I don't believe you are deaf or senseless." She went over, lifted him up and set him on the bedside. Katherine pulled his gown over his head, then with shirt and britches she dressed him as one would dress a baby. After they had found shoes for him, she took a wet cloth and washed his face. She brushed the tangled curls and made him stand for inspection. "These are the things that you must start doing for yourself. I believe you have become spoiled, and I won't allow a smart boy like you to remain helpless." Taking his hand she led him down the stairs and into the hall. Finding no one there, they went through the kitchen and out the back door to find Molly on a back porch, stringing slices of apple to dry for winter. Seeing Jamie with Katherine seemed to surprise her.

"Jamie and I are going to look around the plantation. I promised I would take him with me last night in front of Payton, and there was no objection."

"Nay, 'tis good for the child to get out; 'tis a shame that neither of us have had the mind or the heart to see to the child. I prayed God that one would come to help the boy. 'Tis good ye'er here, Miss, for the boy and the master. Master has gone down to the tobacco sheds to see to the stripping of the leaves and the packing into hogsheads. He said fer me to send word when ye were up and had eaten a bite. In the main hall on the side-board ye will find the morning meal. Perhaps ye would feed the boy if ye can get him to eat. He does like the preserves and bread with a sip of milk sometimes."

All this time Jamie had stood quietly watching the chickens pecking in the yard, seemingly unaware of what was being said.

When Katherine took his hand to lead him back into the hall, he came as if by rote. On the board was a loaf of fresh bread, a dish of berry preserves, some scrambled eggs, a dish of fried pork tenderloin, cheese, and a small pitcher of milk. All had been covered by a clean white cloth to keep out the flies.

"Mmmm, look at this," she told Jamie. "Let's share a plate, You sit down and I will get our food. Is this your little mug? I bet Molly put it out for you. Where did you get such a perfect little mug? I would like to have one just like it, only a bit larger, from which to drink my milk." Playing a game she used to play with their cook's little girl, Katherine broke a slice of bread into several small pieces and put a bit of meat and cheese on two of the pieces. "This one is yours, and this is mine," she said, taking one. "You didn't eat yours. You must so I can fix us one with the preserves." She held it up to him and he opened up his mouth and let her put it in. "Now we need a drink of milk." When she fixed their next bite with preserves, she pushed it to his side of the plate. She picked up his arm and looked at it, "I don't see anything wrong with this arm; let's see if you can get your bite this time." With that she got her own and ate it with much lip-smacking. To her surprise he reached over and got the bite and put it in his mouth. "Now we need another drink of milk. Here, I'll bet you can hold your own cup; of course, I knew you could. " Talking, fixing them bites, and handing him

61

his cup she continued with him through the meal. She was much encouraged by his attention to the process, even though he remained expressionless. With a clean linen napkin, she wiped first his mouth then her own. As she helped him from the bench at the table, where they had been sitting with their back to the door, she was startled to see Payton standing there. "Well, good morning, sir, we were just finishing our morning meal. We were going to look for you on our trip around the plantation."

"Wait here for a few minutes while I get our horses saddled; we can see more on horseback. Seeing you dressed thus I assume you ride."

"I was the champ of Whitehall Square in my younger days; it should come back to me. Jamie can ride with me unless you prefer not. We will await you on the front porch."

Payton brought the horses around and helped her to mount before lifting Jamie up to her. They followed him out of the fort and into the compound, where women and children were involved in the activities of putting up food for winter, stocking the wood piles, and preparing shelters and feed for the animals. Payton described the purpose of several outbuildings along the way. He stopped to speak with every person who took notice of their passing, calling them by name and making her familiar with the trade or craft of husband or father. The men, he explained, were working to get the tobacco ready to load. Everyone had a kind word for Jamie, telling him it was good to see him out, and Payton could sense their approval of a lady who would take time for the poor child.

At the tobacco sheds Payton dismounted and helped them down to watch. He explained that as the tobacco was cut from the fields it was hung on poles under the sheds to dry for about six or eight weeks, according to the humidity. It was then stripped from the poles and packed into the hogsheads for shipping. Hogsheads were being made to the right of where they stood and Katherine watched the skilled hands take the wooden panels and quickly turn them into wire-rimmed barrels. The sun shining on the dried tobacco leaves gave them a golden glow.

When she expressed this thought, Payton told her it was the closest thing to gold that Virginia had produced so far.

When they remounted, Payton lead them in a wide circle around the plantation buildings, pointing into the distance at some of the boundary markers to give her a sense of his holdings. Then they rode along the river to the dock where the tobacco would be loaded. Jamie, sitting in front of her, did turn his head now and then to look about. She was glad to see him taking notice of the world around him and felt that was a good sign. As they headed back to the settlement, Katherine told Payton she had decided to stay and be his wife. Becoming very business- like, she told him that her father had put aside a dowry for her, and though she did not know the amount, she knew it would compare with the amount usually given. She would write to her father's barrister in London and have that transferred to him.

Payton, extremely relieved by her decision, had doubted there would be a dowry; he marveled again at his good fortune. "I am honored that you have chosen to stay. I will do all that is within my power to keep you from regretting that decision. Can you be ready for a ceremony at four o'clock this evening? Since Molly is considered witless by some, and they know her quarters to be outside my home, you can see there is danger to your reputation in every night that passes."

"I will be ready by four, sir. Would you permit me to use your bath chamber? I will be well out of your way before you need use it."

"I think, my lady, the bath chamber is part of the meager bargain for which you have just settled. I will spread the word and find some help in making further arrangements. The main meal will be postponed until after the wedding. This calls for enough food and drink for a grand celebration."

At a quarter to the hour of four, potter Ben, whom she had met at the evening meal on the night before, was there with Payton's chaise to escort Katherine to the tiny chapel. Molly had helped her draw water for the bath and get ready. Now she stood

63

before Molly in the white dress, the silver threads adding a magic sparkle. Her shoes were embroidered pantofles. Tiny pink and white roses, (borrowed from a summer hat) peeked through the mass of golden curls atop her head. A natural radiance added the finishing touch to the fairy tale illusion that Katherine presented.

"Aye, Miss, 'tis a sight to behold, ye are, a picture in that dress. I bless the ship that brought ye to us, fer we all need the hope and the beauty ye bring. I thank ye too for letting me wear this silk waistcoat. I feel like a queen, I do."

Potter Ben led her down the aisle amidst the murmuring aah's of a crowd caught up in fanciful delight. Payton, in doublet and knee-breeches of black satin, the cuffs of the doublet turned back to show a fine linen shirt with embroidered cuffs and collar, stood spellbound as the vision that was to be his wife walked toward him. In that moment he realized he had never known a woman of more beauty and perfection. With that realization came the intense fear that she could become too precious. A vow that he had made to himself long ago slammed and bolted the door to his heart.

Katherine, walking toward the man that her heart had recognized as her destiny, saw the warm approval in his eyes turn suddenly cold. His rejection seemed to be aimed at her, and though he quickly recovered with a smile, the sting stayed with her throughout the ceremony and the feasting afterward. Reverend Swann, minister to the Hundred, was a kind and gentle man whom Katherine liked immediately. She felt guilty for her deception when he spoke her name during the ceremony as Katherine Lawrence. After the ceremony the women of the plantation came forth with the traditional bride's gift, a bread peel, significant of domestic utility and plenty. In accepting the long-handled, wooden shovel used to place food well back into the oven, Katherine felt as if she had been accepted among them. Having moved again to the long house, the eating, drinking, and celebrating was carried into the night. Ale and wine flowed freely and as tongues loosened, the people of the plantation became more comfortable and open with her. For the first time in her life she felt as if she had become part of a large and caring family. Payton, ever attentive and near, finally called for one last toast. Followed by jocularity and catcalls, Payton lead her to where the chaise stood and helped her up. The drink had washed away the austerity she had sensed within him earlier; passion and lust were now apparent in his eyes. Katherine shivered in anticipation, the wine having calmed her own fears of what was to come.

Molly had returned early with Jamie and had the bed turned down on fresh clean sheets. A faint scent of lavender floated in the air. Katherine, hurrying straight to the bath chamber, found that Molly had unpacked some of her things and placed her finest nightgown there, it too freshened with lavender.

Katherine, having heard descriptions from the girls on ship of what she could expect, stripped, washed herself with the scented soap, and put the gown on. Her feelings now were a mingle of fear, excitement, and shame. Maybe the shame was for the excitement, or maybe it was because she was now required to do that which had, until this day, been forbidden. She stood before the closed door for a few moments, gathering the courage to open it and walk into Payton's room. She was thankful he had left only one low candle to dimly show her the way to the opposite side of the bed from where he lay waiting.

She crawled in on her side and lay there timidly waiting for him to guide her through this consummation, trusting that he would treat her gently and respectfully.

"Katherine, have you been with a man before?" He thought it likely she had, but like most women would pretend she had not. "Do you know what to expect?"

"I have not been with a man, but some of the girls on the ship talked about it. I can only beg your patience until I learn what you would have me do to please you."

Payton felt a softening of his heart and having found her to be forthright in other matters, decided to proceed as with a virgin. "This will not be a pleasant experience for you. Indeed it

65

will most likely be painful, for there is within you a membrane that must be broken." Payton reached over and began to caress her body, hoping to soothe away some of the tension. Moving closer to her he pulled her up against him, holding her and stroking her hair, her cheek, and the curves of her neck. Laying her back he began following his strokes with light kisses, stopping to savor the softness and cleanliness of her skin. "You smell wonderful. It's been so long since I have held a woman close and never one of such clean habit." Deft hands fondled their way through the first button of her gown. With light touches of hands and mouth he moved through one after another of the buttons giving attention to every inch of soft, scented flesh in between. Katherine's body responded to his every touch; unknown urges consumed her; she was filled with an impatience that silently begged him for more, more of what, she knew not. Payton had gradually worked loose the pearl buttons that separated his lips from firm breasts and taut nipples. Katherine gasped and moaned softly at the sensations that ran through her body when his tongue traced circles around her nipples. She had never known such ecstasy. Her reaction was fuel to a smoldering fire in Payton's depraved body, an explosive throbbing in his groin was ignited at her gasps, and burst into flames of desire that swept past all mind and all reason. Losing himself in the demands of his own passion, he had a vague sense of sliding the gown up while his mouth lustfully devoured the hard nipples. He no longer owned the body that was now on top of her, wallowing in the warm moistness of flesh against flesh. Against his will, her moans created a power that drove his organ to seek that place of fulfillment, pushing, thrusting, and tearing through. With passion quickly spent he realized with a heartsick feeling that he had lost all control and she, thinking this her duty, had submitted unflinchingly to a brutal rape. Payton put out his hand to touch her cheek and found it wet with silent tears. Her body recoiled as if expecting another onslaught. "Katherine, I am truly sorry. My needs were greater than my reason and I acted in a beastly manner. I hope you can forgive me. You may take the candle to the chamber if you wish I will ask no more of you tonight."

Katherine, her passion having been left wanting and her body sorely used, was mortified. She lay trembling in confusion and pain until she could get her wits together enough to move to the chamber. With the door closed she released the sobs that choked her, and she gave way to renewed anger at a God who had struck her yet again with an unsuspecting blow. The burning pain inside her, the messy wetness, and the shocking let-down were degrading. Taking the cloth she had used earlier, she bathed the tears from her eyes, and washed between her legs. She was not surprised to find the bloody stains on the cloth. She wondered if she would recover and heal before he made new demands on her body. As a measure of defense, she put her underwear back on and leaving the chamber, she found her way to the bed she had slept in the night before.

Payton lay in confusion also. He was a man who had learned to keep a tight reign on passion and emotion. This woman had a power over him that frightened him. When she came out and moved silently into the other room he felt a disappointment, but considering his beastly assault he could hardly blame her. Still, this had to be mended, for he wanted a son and he already ached again for her body. On the morrow he would start over with this woman. By then he would be sober and thinking with his head. When he was seventeen, he had learned the folly of allowing a woman to become too precious. There is no pain like that of watching the woman you love marry your older brother, him being heir to the family fortune and her with no say in the arrangements. At the same time, he had learned that there is no fool like a man caught in the silver web of passion. In this land he could not afford to let his emotions rule his head. Here a man's life and often the lives of others, depended on him keeping his senses. A man who kept himself clear of attachments, was more apt to keep his senses. His hide too.

67

Chapter 9

Payton awoke before daylight and desire flooded through him. He got up and walked into the bedroom where a mass of golden curls were all that could be seen of the woman he had married. Laying back the cover he gently slid his hands under her to pick her up and carry her back to his bed. She awoke with a start and upon awareness, her face showed the remembered pain and degradation. He gave her a soft kiss on the cheek and whispered a "shhh" in her ear. Speaking softly and picking her up at the same time, he began, "My lady, I cannot leave you this morning until we come to an understanding about last night and about our marriage as well." Reaching his bed he held her to him with one hand, bringing up a knee to support her while he flipped back the covers to lay her down. Scarlet spots on the white sheets stared up at him and confirmed the truth of her claim. His respect for her deepened and feelings of guilt reminded him that he had betrayed her trust in him on the night before. His desire to ravish her was replaced with a desire to regain her esteem. He laid her down gently and got in beside her. Propped up on an elbow he began, "Katherine, again I beg your forgiveness for the pain and violation you must have suffered last night and though my passion overcame my control, there is no painless way to go about the taking of a woman's virginity. 'Tis natural that your body guards the sacred place of life within you. It does not give way easily to the first intrusion. For too long I have denied the needs of my own body. Add to that the strong drink and the beauty, the softness, and the scent of that which was before me. My reactions though inexcusable were as much as one could expect from any man under such circumstances. Today is a new day and we will start it with new understandings. You and I have found it convenient to become married, each for our own reasons. My reasons were plain to you from the beginning, so I expect that your body will be available for my own natural urges and the procurement of heirs.

In return I offer you my name, my home, and my deepest respect. I find you to be a lady in the truest sense of the word. You are everything a man could want and more. To the best of my ability, I will protect you and keep you in a manner comparable to any lady in this colony. I know not what you expect from me, but love is the one thing that I am incapable of giving. I hope you can accept me for what I am willing to offer. Do you have expectations of me that you would like to bring up at this time?" When Katherine shook her head 'no,' he continued. "Then I would again like to claim my right to your body, perhaps you would remove the clothing so that I might enjoy the sight as well as the other pleasures."

Katherine, with a new realization of what this marriage meant to Payton, detached herself, in mind, from the situation. She got up, stripped, and lay back down, giving him her body to do with as he pleased. The passion that he had aroused in her on the night before would not be twice fooled. The love that she had thought would grow and bind them together was apparently one-sided. The weight of uncertainty that bore down on her was heavier than Payton's body. The pain of his encroachments on her body was overwhelmed by the desolation she felt. She was still alone, now in a place so far from the few who at least cared if she lived or died. When Payton finished and left to help with the tobacco, Katherine had a good cry. Being alone was something she had learned to cope with. She had learned that tears could release the pressure, but the battle with despair was a battle of wits. Her mind could take her deeper into it or out of it. She had already seen where her mind and education could be put to use in this place. She needed to get dressed and go talk to the Reverend Swann about one of her ideas. But first she must do something about the sheets, for she couldn't leave that to Molly. Within an hour she had washed and dressed, got Jamie up, and put the sheets to soak. She was embarrassed for Molly to see them, but the kind woman insisted that she take Jamie and go on about her business, declaring that by nightfall she would have them back on the bed.

Reverend Swann was down on hands and knees clipping herbs from the garden beside his tiny cottage. As she approached with Jamie he arose and came to greet her. "'Tis a pleasure to see you again Lady Montgomery. Good morning, Jamie. Good to see the boy getting out."

"Reverend Swann, I have come to ask you about using the chapel to hold classes for the children of the plantation. I would like to begin teaching them to read and write. If you have no objection, I thought that from ten to twelve on week-day mornings might be the best time. That would give the children time to finish their morning chores. How do you feel about us using the chapel? Do you think that the parents would agree to release the children for two hours each morning?"

"I think this is a wonderful idea; surely they have seen the importance of education since moving here and having to handle all their affairs through letters. At the moment I can't think of anything that takes place during those hours in the chapel. The prayer bells sound at ten and four. The ten o'clock bell could serve to announce school, and we could start classes each day with a prayer. If it pleases you to begin next week, I will announce it at the Sunday meeting and we will see how they respond."

"Would you also announce that I will be available on week-day afternoons at two o'clock to write letters for anyone who has need of this service. The letters can be business or just to let someone at home know how we fare here. I know there must be many a person back home wondering about a loved one, and many here who would like to relieve the minds of loved ones at home. Reverend, I appreciate you supporting me in teaching the children. I will see what I can beg and borrow in the way of supplies with which to begin. I thank you for your time, and I will let you get back to your work."

"Lady Katherine, I am pleased with both of the services that you are suggesting. You are a godsend to this plantation in more ways than one. I will be here to help you in any way I can. Feel free to use any of the books from my library, and perhaps I can come up with some of the things you will need. Paper is dear and you won't find much of it around."

"I will be taking advantage of your kind offer and again I thank you. I intend to bring Jamie to the classes in the hope that he will come out of this malady or shock that has left him speechless. Have you ever had experience with such as this? Can you give me any suggestions as to how to help him?"

"No dear, 'tis beyond anything I have experienced, but we will give it our prayers and you will be guided to do the right things. I do know that love is a powerful healer and since it was the loss of a mother's love that helped to bring it on, then perhaps a mother's love could help restore him to health."

Jamie had stood beside her with his hand in hers throughout the conversation, seemingly unaware of anything around him. At times his attention seemed closer to the surface than others. She had noticed that children seemed to get his attention. So did words and actions directed to him by name, especially when they included touching. Katherine felt sure the classes would be good for him. As they walked back through the compound, they took time to examine the buildings that stored the foodstuff. The central storehouse was being filled with shelled corn, dried beans, dried fruit, crocks of foods being cured in brine, and hogsheads of foods that had probably been purchased from passing ships. The smokehouse had meat and fish hanging from the walls and rafters. The dirt floor was packed with oils from their dripping. Rough boards formed tables where great slabs of meat laid, being cured with salt. The smell of the meat was not unpleasant or rank, and there was a coolness about the thick-walled building even though the days were still warm. Rustic steps led up to a second level where nuts were laid out to dry. Onions, herbs, and things Katherine did not recognize hung from walls and sat in corners. On the outside of the building, animal skins had been stretched over hewn boards and nailed to the exterior walls to dry. A woman who Katherine remembered being called Nellie had taken the time to explain some of what was going on and to show them the hold, where cabbage and

71

root vegetables that needed to be kept cool were being put back in a dug-out place in a bank that rose up behind the smokehouse. By the time Katherine visited and talked with those who were working to put food by, she had a real respect for the people of Montgomery's Hundred.

As they made their way home, Katherine began thinking of other things she could do to make herself useful without taking away from Molly's established routines. She suspected it was routine that had kept Molly from losing her battle with depression. One thing she had noticed was Jamie's need of new clothing. Other than night rails his wardrobe was meager and outgrown. She could ask Molly if Payton had any clothes that he no longer wore. Some they could use to make up a wardrobe for Jamie, since he would be getting out more. Another thing she wanted to do was learn to do some of the cooking. Molly seemed to have no real interest in anything. She worked from habit, not joy or purpose, and Katherine suspected that she only ate to keep herself going. The meals so far had reflected this attitude. She wondered also if Payton might like to entertain some of his friends now and then. Today when she had been talking to Reverend Swann, she had thought he would be an interesting person to invite to share a meal. Katherine had always spent a lot of time in the kitchen of their home in Whitehall. The warmth of the fires and the jesting and chatter of the servants had drawn her there. Cooke Della, had been tolerant of her and had allowed her to help with some of the wonderful dishes. Ofttimes Cooke would announce to the family that Katherine had made a certain dish or had a hand in the making. This brought praise and attention to her and of course encouraged her to do more. When her father had died and her mother had become involved with Mr. Barlow she had no one but the servants to turn to. After she lost her mother to the laudanum, the servants were the only family she had. She could see now that all of the time she spent with them, giving a hand here or there, may have taught her things that would be useful for the life she had now chosen.

72

Near the entrance to the stockade that surrounded Payton's home was a big tree with a sturdy, low-growing limb that Katherine thought perfect for a swing. As she and Jamie rested there for a few minutes, potter Ben came by and stopped to pass a few words. After telling him about the classes for the children, and of her desire to help any who needed letters written, Katherine mentioned that the limb was perfect to hold a swing for Jamie and the other children.

"Aye, 'tis a good and safe place for them to play. Wait here and I will be right back, for I have just that which is needed to make a proper swing," he said.

In just a few minutes he was back with rope and two boards with holes drilled in each end to pass the rope through and make a seat. Ben cut the rope into two and threw an end of each across the limb and climbed up to attach them. With Katherine on the ground to hold the swings at the right height, they soon had two perfect swings, hanging side by side, ready to be tried out. Seating Jamie in one of them, she helped him clench his fist around the rope and bid him hold on while she pushed him, slowly at first then higher as she saw that he was holding on fine. Potter Ben, standing in front to check the balance of the swing, was sure he saw a softening, almost a smile, on the little stoic face as Katherine pushed him higher. 'Twould be good to have the bits of happy news to tell the family at the midday meal today, he thought.

As the last of the tobacco was carried in hogsheads to the river dock, the men continued to jest with Payton about his wedding night, telling him he looked like the cat that had gotten the cream and that they would have sent someone to England before now to bring him a woman if they had known how much it would improve his temperament. Most of them had worked through the midday meal as they were so near finished. When the potter's son, Dan, came back to find them sitting around talking, he began to relate the news of Katherine and her plan to teach in the chapel and to write letters for anyone on the plantation. He also told the story of the swings and how the

73

child Jamie had surely been close to smiling at being pushed in the swing.

Payton had mixed feelings as he walked toward the house dripping with water from the river. When weather permitted and the river wasn't too muddy, it had become a habit with Payton and some of the others to jump in the river and rinse off the sweat and dust after work. He was pleased with all that Katherine intended to do for the tenants and all that she was doing for Jamie. What bothered him was the way she had arranged all this without a word to him, leaving him to find out from a tenant. She was not like any woman he had known before. There was about her an air of independence and he wasn't sure whether that was good or bad. As they sat down to eat he commented on the things he had heard and told her that they were fine things she was doing. Then he suggested that from now on she discuss things of importance with him first, in case there should be some reason why they weren't feasible. Katherine sensed that Payton was a bit disturbed about her making decisions and putting them into action without mentioning them to him first. She wasn't sure whether it was a blow to his pride or a sincere concern that she didn't yet know enough about the plantation and its people to jump into their affairs. "Had our relationship been less strained and had I not been seeking a distraction from the despair of facing a marriage where love will have no chance to grow, I'm sure I would have confided in you first."

Payton was sorry that time and circumstance had not allowed them to have a normal courtship with a chance to become better acquainted. Nothing he could say would undo last night, so he finished his meal in silence.

Chapter 10

Katherine's life on the plantation soon began settling into a routine. Payton awoke most every morning with the desire to use her body. At night and on Sundays or days when he wasn't out working he would also desire her. Either he was a lustful man or he was relentless in getting an heir.

Katherine had loved Payton from the minute she first looked into his eyes and for those few precious moments that he needed her she could enjoy his nearness, even hope that his lust would turn to love in time. Her body ached to have its own passions sated, but Payton avoided those actions which had first aroused her to want. This left her with passion flooding through her at inconvenient times. Sometimes in the middle of a conversation with him she would be overcome with a desire to be ravished and lose her place in the conversation, other times just watching him go about some task or having him brush against her would bring on a spell of longing. As she continued to hold at bay these feelings, they seemed to grow stronger. Avoiding him did not help; release came only when she became involved in activities which required her full attention and fulfilled her need for purpose and accomplishment.

After Payton left in the morning she took an hour or so at the writing desk in their room to complete preparations for the class or to find literary material of interest to the varied age range of her students. By ten she had finished getting herself ready for the day as well as getting Jamie up, dressed, fed, and to the chapel. There she met with five boys from Payton's 'hundred' and four from the neighboring plantations. Two of those boys were Indian boys who were living with Richard Pace. They spent the hours from ten to twelve learning their letters, and numbers, and reading. By two in the afternoon she and Jamie had eaten the midday meal with Payton and Molly and Katherine had put the boy down for a nap. She took care each time she put Jamie down to hold him to her and assure him of her love for

75

him. Often a vague sense of recognition would come to her in connection with Jamie and then evade her. Looking into his green eyes were almost like looking into her own, and she was often told the child looked enough like her to be her own. Katherine wondered if perhaps it wasn't the aloneness or the wounded spirit of the child that she recognized. She cared deeply for him and could see his improvement day by day. She often saw him smiling at the pranks and jests of the boys in class. She could see him thinking and involved in the stories they discussed, and she felt he was on the verge of trying to write or draw.

While Jamie slept she wrote the letters for those who would come to her. The first week, no one had come, then potter Ben came and the two of them could be seen with heads bent over the letter on the porch. Next Ben's son Dan had come. Katherine had felt so sorry for him as he tried to express his feelings to his girlfriend in England through Katherine. Stuttering and stammering with red face, he was unable to say his true feelings through a second person. It was then that Katherine had suggested that Dan come to her classes and learn to write for himself. She told him that he had a wonderful mind and he owed it to himself and his family to get enough education to handle the affairs of the family in years to come. Unless, of course, he would be content to let his younger brother Dennis do that. Dan had been in her class the next day and every day since. If no one came to have a letter written or if she finished early, she sewed on the clothes for Jamie that Molly had helped her cut from Payton's castoffs.

Payton and Molly had been in the habit of making the midday meal their main meal and then eating any leftovers for their evening meal. Katherine had begun to experiment with the memory of Cooke Della's procedures and the spices she had been carrying to her cousin in Plymouth. Often she would have a spicy pasty made from dried apples or other dried fruit to add to the assortment of leftovers. Other times she would create new dishes from the leftovers, putting them together into a shepherd's

76

pie, a pottage, or custard and using some of the dried herbs to give them a new flavor. At the French school she attended they often used herbs and sauces to dress up the simple fare. She would think back and try to guess the ingredients in some of her favorites. By trying a tiny bit of the herbs at a time, and then tasting, she had come up with some fine dishes. Her failures had gone into the slop bucket for the pigs, so had not been wasted. Payton noticed and complimented her on any changes, whether to do with food, Jamie, home, or school. Jamie took midday and evening meals with them and had become adept at feeding himself. He also responded, even though silently, to Payton's comments and acknowledgments. She had begun to have Reverend Swann over to dine with them on Sunday and Thursday evenings.

At those times when Payton needed to retire to his study, or was away for a meeting of the council, Katherine and the Reverend had some exciting discussions over a game of chess, which was often left on the board to continue on their next evening together. The Reverend, in some ways, reminded Katherine of her grandfather who had lived with them for several years before his death. She had found in the Reverend a good friend and one in whom she could confide her most personal thoughts. She had told him that the death of her brother in the duel, followed by the death of her father and the situation with her mother, had left her with little faith in God. He had explained that God often places us where such trials will strengthen us and help us acquire the qualities we will need for our purpose in life. After a reasonable time of mourning we must seek the lessons from the trials we have drawn, so that those who gave to our spiritual growth will not have given for naught. Then we must move on toward our spiritual potential. He often found just the right opening in their conversations to plant the seed of a spiritual thought and Katherine tended those she could accept, giving them back to him in their maturity. Reverend Swann was liberal in his personal beliefs; his God was not a man in the sky. Once he had told her that the jealous, wrathful God was a man-made God, created in the image of man.   Another time, when she had mentioned sin, he had explained to her that sin was an old archery term which meant that one had 'missed the mark.' He had gone on to say that man is not punished for his sins but by his sins.   Reverend Swann's God was a loving presence within each of us, saying yea and verily to us in all that we believe, whether those beliefs be constructive or destructive.

Sometimes he would explain passages from the Holy Book, telling her that much was said that was not meant to be taken literally.   An example that made Katherine see the stories of Jesus in a new light was the parable of the talons, where each version has Jesus saying that to those who have, more shall be given and to those who have not, more will be taken away. "'Tis all in the belief," Reverend Swann said. "To those who believe themselves to be blessed, thankful for all that the Lord has given to them, more shall be given. To those who believe they have been short-changed, seeing only that which they have not and envying that which others have, even more will be taken away." Through the Reverend Swann, Katherine was able to dismiss old beliefs that had been born out of misunderstanding and accept new beliefs that excited her as they substantiated a knowing within her and gained magnitude with contemplation.   He stimulated her to begin building a new philosophy for living and to question that which had been unquestionable before.

Payton, in their conversations on the porch or in front of the fire each evening, stimulated her thinking also, for he was absorbed in the human condition and what could be done to improve it. As Katherine began to believe more and more that we are all one, empowered by the same source to recognize the divine spirit in all life, she wondered if the human condition wasn't dependent on the spiritual condition. Not on the external signs that men judge as moral and pious, but on the inner growth of love, understanding, and acceptance.

The tenants had gotten more used to her and had become more comfortable with her presence there. More and more of them were coming to her for letters to be written. She laughed with them as they humorously exaggerated the riches and the hardships of the new country in the letters they had her write. She cried with them when the letter was to break the news of death or tragedy in a family. She wrote letters to the girlfriends of shy men and boys like Dan, who squirmed and turned red-faced through the whole process. The girls who had her write to their boyfriends were better at expressing themselves and the subjects were usually less intimate in nature. She hoped that the limitations of having someone else write their words would fill others with the desire to learn to write. Katherine sensed that this country, which seemed to be growing in separate units because of the plantation system established here, would be a long time in establishing schools and would require mothers who could teach their children at home. She intended to be prepared with an argument for the girls to attend her classes by the time they started again after the planting season. In the meantime she was suggesting to the boys that they share the things they were learning with any members of the family who were receptive.

Through the children in her classes, Katherine was learning much about the families and the people of Jamestowne. The two Indian boys, Nantauquas and Chanco, were obedient and intelligent. Chanco, being younger, was a lovable child, eager to learn and to please. He was considerate of Jamie and often waited to help him when the boys took their break and went to relieve themselves at the toilets. Chanco was ever amazed by the golden curls of Jamie and Katherine. He often would reach out and touch their hair, almost with a reverence. The "Deaf Pew," which allowed the hard of hearing to sit in front during church services, had become the dunce seat and the boys would go into a fit of laughter each time Katherine ordered one of them to the front for not listening or for distracting the others. Neither of the Indian boys had ever required discipline, although there was an insolence or cunning attitude about Nantauquas that led Katherine to believe he could be a danger to the Pace family in the event of an Indian uprising. Perhaps to Montgomery's

Hundred also, for he was familiar with the routines of both places and showed an uncommon interest in the weaponry of the tenants at their hundred.

As Christmas neared the tiny chapel began to be so cold inside that the children could hardly concentrate on their lessons. The week before Christmas Katherine dismissed them from classes until after the holidays. She had talked to Payton and he had promised to get them a better source of heat for the building by the time they came back after the holidays.

Having extra time she and Molly began baking gifts for the tenants, using much of her small store of spices. They looked forward to giving them treats that they had not enjoyed since leaving home. She, Molly, and Jamie worked together on making gifts for the children of the plantation. Taking from some of her less appropriate clothing, they were able to make some pretty little dolls for the small girls and fancy bonnets for the older girls. Again, Payton's castoffs provided material for caps, gloves, or leggings for the boys. Payton also had gifts put back that had come in on various ships and as the time grew near there was a festive air about the 'hundred' and excitement on the faces of the children.

On the night before Christmas, the boards were set for a great feast in the compound. Katherine, at the unusual request of Payton, dressed again in the green dress she had worn the day she had first met Payton. As she came out of the bath chamber after putting her hair into a chignon, Payton awaited her with a long, velvet-covered box. From it he took a diamond and emerald necklace with earrings to match. He fastened the necklace around her neck, turned her around, and kissed her gently on the lips.

"This seemed like a good time to give my present to you. These jewels belonged to my mother, Priscilla Montgomery. She was fair of skin and hair as you, and though her eyes were blue, they took on a green hue when she wore these jewels. In many ways you remind me of her. The way you carry yourself and present yourself as a lady at all times; also the respect you show for all people, no matter what their station in life. I admired that in her and I admire it in you also. I think she would have approved of you in every way and would have wanted these passed to you. I want you to see this gift as a token of my appreciation for the many things you do for me, for Jamie, for Molly, and the people of my hundred. Merry Christmas, dear. I'll leave the earrings for you to fasten."

Katherine was stunned and delighted. The value of the gift was immeasurable, but the sentiment behind it was worth more to her than the material value of the perfect stones set in gold filigree. Hope sprang within her that fate had intervened to change his belief that he was incapable of love. What she had seen in his eyes, if not love, was an affection close to love. As she put the earrings on and positioned them so they didn't pinch, she savored the moment. "Payton Montgomery, you were meant for me and I for you. I pray you are beginning to see that as clearly as I have from the beginning," she said to herself. Then she remembered that all she had to give him were a few little homemade articles of clothing and plum pudding.

On Christmas day it was required that all colonists attend the parish church at Jamestowne, so the plantation feast and celebration had to end early in order for them to arise in time to get the farm animals taken care of and make the trip.

The women of Montgomery's Hundred had outdone themselves in creating food for this occasion, and the mood was one of festivity and excitement. Payton had a wagon load of gifts for the tenants, mostly practical tools, weapons, and equipment for the men. For the women there was cloth and sewing materials, cooking utensils, blocks of sugar, and spices. The children had received their toys and candy first, so they were happily discovering what everyone else had gotten. Katherine was happy to see that Payton had purchased cloth for Molly and her, spices to replenish their depleted stock, and lots of paper and materials for her classes. Not since she was a child had Katherine enjoyed such a wonderful Christmas. Having learned to do without so many of the things she took for granted made her more appreciative of the gifts of sweet-smelling soaps, the candles, and the hand-loomed and woven goods that the women of the hundred had given her. She was surprised at the talent and artistry among them, and she wondered when they had found time for the elaborate but practical gifts they shared with her and the others. As she looked around her, she realized that the ocean that lay between them and the rest of the world had created a sense of family that transcended class or coterie. Again she felt a sense of belonging that filled and warmed the empty places within her. A tear dropped from each eye as she bowed her head for a moment to say a personal thank you and ask that a special blessing be bestowed upon these loving people.

Chapter 11

They traveled to Jamestowne the next morning in canoes and small boats. Katherine enjoyed the trip up river and was surprised to find it much shorter by river than by land. After a full morning of church services they were allowed an intermission at midday. They gathered at the noon-house where a great fire burned and before which they dined on sweetbreads. There Katherine was able to visit with the women who had come over on the ship with her. Charlotte had changed from child to woman and seemed to be happy with her choice of the young man she had met on that first day. She stood on tiptoe to whisper in Katherine's ear that she was again with child and that this child would be welcomed into a big family who had already begun making clothes and cradle for it. The others, some seemingly content, some disillusioned, were much as they had been on the ship. Those of a nature to accept and make the best of things were doing that; those who were of a nature to find fault were doing that. Doris had married the keeper of the tavern and was said to be carrying on as if she had never left the streets of London. Bertha was there with her John, and Katherine liked him immediately; he was a sensitive, intelligent man who was several years older than Bertha.

When Katherine returned to Payton's side she was introduced to the Governor and Mrs. Wyatt, a seemingly proper couple who were trying not to slight any of the colonists during this short recess. Elizabeth Hamor was there with a friendly smile for Katherine, but the bell for afternoon services rang before they had time to really visit.

Katherine dreaded going back for the afternoon services. At the chapel on their 'hundred,' Reverend Swann spoke as a humble teacher. He used the words of Jesus and other master teachers to help his listeners form ideas about God that were healthy and loving. He saw God as a power for good, and all God's children as expressions of the One Power. When describing us as being created in the image of God, he had once used the James River as an illustration. He poured a cup of water from the river into a clear glass decanter. "Just as this cup of water from the river contains all the elements of that mighty river, you and I have all the elements of God," he had said. The end purpose of all his sermons was to give his parishioners the spiritual tools they needed to rediscover their own divinity and their own power through a personal relationship with God. His studies constantly took him to new levels of understanding, and his enthusiasm in sharing these insights was exciting and uplifting to his congregation.

The attitude of Reverend Wright in Jamestowne was one that suggested the only path to God was through worthy mediators such as himself. He used the words of the Bible to demean and create guilt. During the morning services, Katherine had regressed to the little child of yesteryear, looking at the toes of her Sunday shoes, and silently crying out, "No, no, no, this is not right, why are you teaching all these people to believe this way?" Now as Reverend Wright began the afternoon services with more of the same, Katherine, in a flash of awareness and pity from somewhere deep within, offered a prayer: "Forgive him God, for he knows not what he does. He knows not the fear and the guilt that will have to be unlearned, somewhere, sometime, by his followers and himself." Reverend Wright did know the distance that many of the crowd had traveled to attend the Christmas services and he dismissed them at an early hour. All were weary, and upon arrival at the 'hundred,' quickly took care of the most necessary of the evening chores. As a group, they again dined on the remains of their feast of the night before, then quickly adjourned to their own homes. In the parlor, by the fire, Payton and Katherine took an hour or so to talk and relax before bed. When Katherine told Payton of her feelings during the church services, he revealed some things about himself that she had not known.

"It was my mother's desire that I go into the ministry since I was the second son and she saw in me qualities she felt one needed to be effective in the ministry. Having a small fortune of her own, she set aside most of it for my schooling and my upkeep during the years of learning and becoming established. After I moved through the basic studies and then completed theology, I knew that I had to begin again and reformulate my beliefs. I had a teacher, Dr. Vachel, who continues even now to influence my thinking. Reverend Swann is also a student of Dr. Vachel. There was about Vachel an air of love and mysticism, almost what one would expect Jesus to be like, had he lived to become elderly. The students either loved him or hated him. Those who were afraid to question their beliefs felt threatened by his logic and intelligence in discerning the literal from the spiritual in God's messages. He had devoted his whole life to the study of the ancient holy books of all the major religions, scriptures that were compiled hundreds of years before our Bible. It was his belief that sometime after Jesus was twelve, he also studied these holy books, along with his cousin, John the Baptist. According to Vachel, everything that was said and taught by Jesus was first recorded among the ancient books of other religions. Vachel saw, he believed that Jesus saw also, the common threads of truth that run through every major religion. These he called the real truths, given by one God to all men. The differences that sprang up between religions, he saw as the expansions and elaborations of mankind. With a deep sadness, Vachel would point out that the God-given truths designed to bring the world together in unity were used, through misunderstanding, to separate the people from each other and from God."

"But why does each religion think that they are the only one right, and that anyone who believes different is a threat, to be converted or put to death? I noticed this in France and through my studies I saw religion as the direct or the underlying cause of many wars."

"It does seem that any group who believed God to be all powerful would leave such judgments to God, doesn't it? Katherine, all religions are right and all are wrong, just as all parents are right and all are wrong. Ultimately, not one of us can depend on our religion, our parents, or anything outside ourselves to render us our salvation. It is a process of soul-searching and growing spiritually. I have begun to see it as a lifetime journey."

"You sound like Reverend Swann. Did you choose him because of his liberal beliefs, or was it by chance that he ended up here? I have often thought that in England the hierarchy would come down on him for his liberal beliefs."

"I knew Wallace Swann at Cambridge. Later, in London, I began to meet with a group of Raleigh's friends who discussed different philosophies. Swann was one of the leaders in the group. When word got out that we were questioning God's holy word, as given to us by the Crown, we were labeled atheists and our meetings called the 'School of Night.' Wallace decided to leave England when Raleigh was imprisoned the last time. He believed the king feared Raleigh's influence and possibly knew of Swann's outspoken ideas. After traveling and studying with some of the great minds of France and Italy, he ended up here and I was glad to have him. He recently made me aware that the dominant religions in countries all over Europe are suffering dissension. We have begun to get a few groups here, perhaps because of our liberal policy. From the little I know of the groups settling in Virginia, it seems as if they are merely exchanging one dogma for another. I've heard that a group of Puritans intend to establish a colony to the north of us. I worry about any religion that serves to separate one group of people from another. I do believe, however, that for those who have expressed a desire and have opened their minds to the discovery of the spiritual truths, God will always provide beacons of light to guide them."

"Such as Reverend Swann; he has helped me in so many ways. Because I couldn't reconcile what I heard in church with what I felt inside, I was filled with guilt and fear, sure that I must be the only one who dared to question. When the time came that I desperately needed faith, I didn't have enough to see me through; I believed I was being punished.   Reverend Swann is helping me to come to terms with my anger at God and my fear of more punishment. So much of what he says feels right and inspires me to new questions and new answers. His insights have helped me to find peace and joy in my relationship with God. I am truly thankful that he is here for us. I am thankful too that you shared your experience with me. Your friend Dr. Vachel's beliefs make more sense than any explanation I have heard. What is most wonderful about his theory is that it supports our need to question and cull out those beliefs that hinder the evolution of mankind."

"Before we turn in, I must tell you that I will soon have to go away for a week or so. Today Governor Wyatt requested that the council convene at the end of the twelve days of Christmas. There are many changes taking place with the five-year plan that the company has set up for us to follow. The stockholders of the company are trying to get us set up to produce products other than tobacco; it is not good policy to be dependent on one product. I cannot say how long I will be at Jamestowne but potter Dan will see to you and Molly. I will return the day we adjourn."

That night when Payton took her to him she thought it was with a new tenderness, and she allowed herself to believe that he was coming to love her as she loved him.

On New Year's Day, Payton left for the meeting of the council in Jamestowne. By week's end, Katherine realized what an important part of her life he had become. She knew his routine by heart, and at those times that he was usually home she missed him sorely. Word came through one of the tenants who had rowed that day to Jamestowne that Payton would be home by night. A cold rain had set in and she knew not if Payton was prepared for it. Out in the kitchen she had a warm fire and the smell of the supper she was making for him drifted all the way down to the compound. The English were not partial to vegetables and ate them only as a last resort, unless cooked to a mush in a stew or ragout. Katherine had learned to make them a delicious part of their meals and having found fresh greens in the kitchen garden ready for picking, she had wilted a mess and combined them with eggs, cheese, and milk and baked them in a crust with just a pinch of nutmeg. She had picked through the apples in storage, taking those with spots and using the good parts to make a spicy tart. Molly and Jamie had eaten meat and bread left from the midday meal, and both were in bed. Katherine had taken the spinach pie from the oven and had left the tart a few more minutes to brown. With the bread peel she slid the pottery dish to the front of the oven and grabbed the handle of the dish with a potholder. Just as she turned to set it on the kitchen board, the handle broke and the tart fell to the floor, splashing the hot juice on her feet and legs. Somehow in trying to avoid the scalding liquid she stepped on a glob of the tart and her foot slid out from under her. She landed in the floor with one hip in the hot tart. Payton opened the door to the kitchen at that moment and roared in laughter at the sight of her sitting in the middle of such a mess. Then seeing that she was in pain, he helped her up and quickly stripped off the soiled clothes that were holding the heat against her body. With a washpan of cool water and a soft cloth he washed the sticky juice from her skin, finding several small burns on her feet and a large one on her hip. The thickness of dress and underclothes had kept the burn on her hip from going deep, but he wasn't sure about those on her feet. He went to the great room and came back with some salve, which he spread gently on her burns. She could smell the drink on his breath and suspected they had celebrated the adjournment before heading home. He had knelt before her to put the salve on her and now as he became quiet and still, she looked down to see the transparent glow of desire in his eyes as he took in every inch of her naked body. Without a word he stood and picked her up, he carried her into the hall and up the stairs, and laid her on the bed then began taking off his wet clothing. Katherine pulled down the covers and got in beneath them for the room was cold. The way he had cared for her burns and the softness in his eyes had brought passion flooding through her, and now she tried to push it from her by thinking of her ruined supper. Payton got in bed and to her surprise he began as he had on that first night, caressing her body with kisses and nibbles, going back again and again to her breasts where short gasps of breath and soft moans set him on fire. Tonight he wanted to bring her to rapture. He wanted to feel her move against him. He wanted her to know all the pleasure he was capable of giving her. Payton wanted her body, her soul, and her mind to be his completely, and he gave to her all that he had withheld from her. Her soft moans turned to guttural sounds and her hips moved in a rhythmic motion against his face. He brought her to the height of ecstasy and just as that ecstasy pushed her over the edge and turned her into a quivering mass of exposed nerves, he entered her and found that place of longing; then he thrust against it and she rose up with muscles tight around his manhood, squeezing him until he could barely hold back. They were of one mind now, she clawing his hips and crushing herself against him, he pushing to the depths of her being. An animal like wail from her drove him even harder and deeper and in unison the flames of passion burst into a million sparks of rapture and left them spent and quivering in each other's arms.

Katherine, her passion spent, found herself overwhelmed by love and the true oneness that they had shared. Tears of euphoria flowed from her eyes and down her face. Payton holding her and stroking her hair and cheek, felt her tears and tipped her chin up to see that she was crying.

"Why, Katherine, what's wrong? Tell me if I was too rough, if I did anything to cause you distress."

"No darling, I'm crying because I'm so happy, because I love you so and because I now know the meaning of being joined together as one."

"Katherine, forgive me if I have misled you into thinking that my lust was love. With a spiritual love, I do love you and all human kind. I have the highest regard for you as a person and as a beautiful and intelligent woman, but please do not ask me to pretend that which is not possible for me. When I was

89

seventeen, I loved a woman with all my heart. When I went away to school, she fell in love with my brother and they asked me to be best man at their wedding. The next woman that I loved died after being thrown from a horse. Before I had begun to recover from that, my mother died. Two years ago I came home to find my daughter, who was the dearest to my heart of any love I had known, dead and mutilated. Her mother, who had been my friend since childhood, had been strapped to poles and skinned alive. I have no more of that kind of love left in me; if I did I would be afraid to allow it, afraid for the person I loved and afraid for my sanity in losing that person. Anything I have to give, I give freely to you, but love of the kind you desire is not within me to give. Please let us live peacefully together without making impossible demands upon each other."

Chapter 12

A cold wind blew off the river as Carlton made his way to the company compound at Jamestowne. The ship's captain had told him that they kept barracks there for bachelors or men traveling alone. He was taken to a small cot in a line of others just like it. The floor was dirt and the stench of men's unclean bodies mingled with that of vomit, urine, and feces. Carlton longed again for home and all the everyday comforts that he had taken for granted. His trip to find Katherine had turned into an extended nightmare. The ship that he had sailed on had been caught in a storm and due to extensive damage to the rigging had limped into port at Bermuda. There, he had been stranded for more than two months. Now upon arrival at Jamestowne he had been unable to find anyone who had even heard of Lady Katherine Arlington. It frightened him to think of her fate if she was not here in Virginia. She could either be dead or sold to some rich merchant in the West Indies. Carlton walked to the tavern for a meal and a mug. The tavern keeper's wife, being of a friendly nature, inquired as to his travels and was outrageously flirtatious. Her husband seemed to allow her free rein. Carlton asked the woman, called Doris, if she knew of a lady having come to Jamestowne in the past three months, and she told him of a Katherine Lawrence, who had married a gentleman named Payton Montgomery. Her description of the lady sounded as if it could be Katherine, even though the last name was wrong. With directions to the Montgomery Plantation and a small boat hired for the morning, Carlton made his way back to the barracks to let the brew put him to sleep in the coarse lodgings. Carlton would acquaint himself with this Lady Montgomery on the morrow and be back in time to set sail on the Warsaw by the following day. He was more than ready to quit this new world and get back to civilization. That which he might salvage of his inheritance looked better for his having been without anything these many months.

Morning found him with a hired boatman moving upstream to Montgomery's Hundred. The wind was cold and blew against them as they rowed into it. They had passed two docks and were coming up on the third one. A crude sign said "Pace's Pains." The boatman told Carlton of the tobacco production, of the shipping and receiving of goods from the river docks, and he explained how each of these particular plantations was a community unto itself, all using the river as their main source of transportation. He talked of the men who owned the plantations and explained the terms under which a man might acquire land. Those with large tracts had acquired them by providing transportation for others to come to the colony. Usually the plantation owner took responsibility for getting his tenants settled and together they formed a protective community against Indians and starvation. When a man had served out his time as tenant, which the boatman thought to be about seven years, then he was granted land of his own. Montgomery's Hundred was one of the most productive and self-sufficient of the lot. Of course, Montgomery had bought into the company earlier, and acquired his property through them. Altogether there were about twenty tracts called hundreds or plantations on the river.

When they had tied the boat and walked to the compound of Montgomery's Hundred, Carlton was surprised to find the place very much like a little English village. A palisade surrounded the whole village while an older stockade enclosed a finer two-story house of rough sawed lumber and windows. Carlton was directed to that house while the boatman was welcomed by the tenants and invited to share with them the midday meal. At the main house, Carlton was met by a sad-looking woman and directed to the chapel where Lady Katherine was to be found.

Katherine had just dismissed her students and they were moving through the door when Carlton walked up. Katherine stopped Chanco on the porch and in spite of his impatience to go, tied the strings to his cap, buttoned the first two buttons that he had left unbuttoned on his coat, and kissed his cheek; then she called for the three older boys to wait for him to catch up.

92

When she saw Carlton walking toward her she could hardly believe her eyes.

"Is it really you Carlton? What a wonderful surprise. Come to the house and join us for our midday meal. Tell me what brings you to the colony and how are things are in London?"

"Katherine Arlington, I came in search of you and found you using another name. I must know what is going on and how you came to marry in such haste."

"Come on, I will explain everything. Carlton, this is Jamie, my stepson," Katherine said as she almost tripped over the boy. "Shake Carlton's hand, love."

Carlton stood for a moment in amazement, as if he couldn't believe his eyes. "Are you sure this isn't your nephew? This boy is Samuel Arlington made over; this boy is his son. Egad, Katherine, surely you must see that no one but Samuel could have fathered this child. Where is his mother and why is he here with you?"

Katherine's heart jumped at the prospect of Jamie's relationship; it took her a full minute to realize the implication of such news. Yet what he was saying rang true. That would confirm the recognition she had felt from the time of her first meeting with Jamie. Maybe something in her had recognized the Samuel in Jamie. The Samuel of many years ago.

"What do you mean, Carlton? I don't understand how Jamie could possibly be Samuel's son."

Jamie, his attention moving from one to the other as they talked, had listened intently from the first mention of Samuel Arlington. He now motioned for Katherine to follow him to the house and into Payton's study. Going to a shelf, he took down an elaborately carved wooden box and handed it to Katherine. She opened it to find it packed with mementos that had apparently belonged to Angie, Jamie's mother. As Katherine looked through the odd assortment of letters and papers, she found a certificate of birth that had been drawn up on regular paper and signed by witnesses. Samuel James Arlington, II, was the name on the certificate.

93

"You really hadn't suspected Katherine? How could you look at that child and not see Samuel? There is only one explanation. The man you married is the same one who killed your brother and took Angela. That was the name of the woman Samuel had been seeing. I knew he was in love with an Angela, who designed costumes for the plays of Shakespeare, and I knew he had begun spending a lot of time with her. He had even mentioned marrying her, asked if I thought his father would ever accept a shepherd's daughter into the family. I thought it was just an infatuation and that in time he would get over her. I never dreamed she would get him killed."

"She was his wife," Katherine said. I remember now. I saw the Certificate of Marriage and Angela Mellon was the name on it. It was hidden in a secret compartment that Samuel had built into his buggy. She was his wife and this is his son, but I do not believe that Payton had anything to do with the death of my brother. There has to be some other explanation. I know Payton Montgomery to be an honorable man. He is my husband and I love him. He will clear this up as soon as he returns. Now, let me see if Molly has our meal ready."

Carlton held out a hand to Jamie and introduced himself as a good friend of Jamie's father. When Jamie shook his hand but said not a word, Carlton looked to Katherine.

"Jamie does not speak," Katherine explained. "He is suffering from the trauma of seeing his mother and sister killed by the Indians. He has not spoken a word in almost two years. You two get washed up there at the basin while I help Molly bring in the food."

The midday meal was their main meal of the day. Today Katherine was grateful that Molly had cooked a good meal in spite of the fact that Payton would not be home. After getting the food to the board with everything Katherine could find in the way of condiments, they sat and returned thanks before resuming their conversation. The addition of Molly at the table changed the subject and Carlton related the story of his trip, the storm, and his stay in Bermuda. He told Katherine that she knew about

94

as much of the news from home as he, since only a few weeks separated their departures. After Molly had brought them a glass of wine to take to the parlor and had taken Jamie to put him down for his nap, they were able to take up where they had left off.

"Katherine, do you realize that Jamie is the heir that your father so wanted, in order to keep the Arlington Estates in his family? I saw him not long before his death, and he expressed his sorrow that Robbie would step in and take all that he had worked to restore. He said that each time the estates had passed to that side of the family, it had taken generations of hard work and a king's ransom to retrieve them from debt and decay. He said he had set up a fund that Robbie could not touch except for repairs and maintenance, but there was no assurance that he wouldn't figure out some way to embezzle from it. Your father hinted that Robbie may have had a hand in Samuel's death and suggested that he had hired someone to look into it. I can't think of a better gift that Samuel could have given his father than this child. It is imperative that we get him back home immediately. An Indian uprising or this winter cold and dampness could take him in the blink of an eye. There are doctors who may be able to help him talk, in England. Also, we must get that Certificate of Marriage before Robbie finds it in the buggy. That is an important part of the proof of Jamie's inheritance. I plan to sail on the Warsaw tomorrow. You must bring the boy and come with me."

"I couldn't leave without seeing Payton. He will explain all this to us but he may not be back for two or three days. He took a small hunting party out to search for fowl and game."

"Katherine, there may not be another ship leaving here for months. In the midst of winter, with the tobacco all shipped, I can't see that it would profit anyone to sail to Virginia before spring planting time. You could leave him a letter and explain the necessity for getting Jamie there before Robbie has a chance to destroy the proof we need and take away funds that are necessary for the upkeep of the properties. This is the last thing you can do for your father and brother. If my suspicions are true, we may also uncover information that will explain the deaths of Samuel and Matthew. That is, if your judgment of this Montgomery chap can be trusted."

"Carlton, what are you saying? My father's death was an accident, wasn't it?"

"You've never thought it strange that a man who had driven his team on that road all his life would lose control and go down an embankment? Katherine, your father was a man who stayed calm in any situation. He always had a good team and he knew how to handle them. He wouldn't have been drinking that heavily and he wouldn't have fallen asleep. Matthew's accident has remained a question in the minds of all who knew him. You and your mother were too distraught to think clearly at the time, and no one wanted to cause you further grief by suggesting any wrong-doing."

"Oh, my God, surely Robbie wouldn't do such a thing. Samuel was like a brother to him, and Father was the same as his own father. I just can't believe him capable of such greed."

"Katherine, you must remember how jealous Robbie was of Samuel. Your father always treated Robbie with kindness, yet he was forever pitting Samuel against his father. Robbie created misunderstandings between Samuel and me so often, I just stopped coming around. Samuel was fed up with Robbie, there at the end, especially tired of financing his every whim. Come to think of it Samuel mentioned that Robbie had been trying to stir up trouble between him and Angela. Said Robbie had been following her and making exaggerated claims against her, suggesting that she was loose with her favors."

"Robbie did try to force himself on me once, when I was about twelve," Katherine said, searching back through her memory to get a grown-up view of Robbie's nature. "I took off my shoe and beat him up, then never gave him another chance to get me alone. But still, as much as I disliked his actions, I always felt sorry for Robbie and so did Samuel."

"Of course, that's what kept Samuel beholden to him, giving him money and including him in all his activities. Robbie's mother saw to it that Matthew felt the proper guilt for being born of the right brother. When Robbie's father was killed at sea, she made Matthew feel responsible for her son. Robbie learned early to use his 'poor cousin routine' to feather a nest within your family. But we have all seen how malicious he could become when that routine was ignored. Remember how insulted he became when asked to do some work around the place, even though you and Samuel were required to do chores? Katherine, you must make a decision and make it quickly. It is up to you to claim Jamie's inheritance and the sooner you get home and get started, the better chance you have of winning it for him. One thing you must do is keep Jamie's presence a secret until you get everything in order, for if Robbie did indeed bring about the death of Samuel and Matthew, Jamie will be in great danger. Should Robbie find out about him, I doubt that an ocean between them could protect the child. We must get Robbie stopped before he takes anything else from your family, including lives."

Carlton returned to Jamestowne to book passage for the three of them. Katherine sat down and wrote Payton a long letter, explaining as best she could her reasons for going. She included her true name and the circumstances of her being brought to Virginia. She asked that he write as soon as possible and explain all that he knew of this whole affair, including how he was involved in her brother's death and the keeping of her brother's wife and child. She told him how Jamie, at the mention of Samuel's name, had shown her the papers that proved he was her nephew and heir to the Arlington Estate. She would need those papers to claim the inheritance for Jamie, but would get them back to Payton as soon as it was settled. She ended by explaining her uncertainty as to their relationship, trying to help him understand her agony in loving him so very much only to face his indifference. When she had finished the five-page letter she felt purged of the many months of pent up emotions, and she knew that, should she return to this place it would be of her own free will and with a clear understanding of the sacrifices required to live here. There would be no more deceptions between Payton and her, and she would come back willing to risk all for the one love of her life; otherwise she would not come back at all.

After writing the letter Katherine tried to explain to Molly why she must go, but Molly became very upset that she was taking Jamie; she kept insisting that Katherine should wait until Payton returned. Katherine then went to Reverend Swann and explained the whole story to him. Katherine had discussed their marital problems with him several times, and Reverend Swann had tried to intervene to no avail. Now as he listened to her story, he thought it right, considering the circumstances of her kidnaping and the boy being her nephew that Katherine should make the decision. He believed it best also that she wait for Payton to return, but, like Carlton, he knew it likely that it would be weeks, if not months, before another ship came upriver at this time of year. The Reverend walked back with her to talk to Molly. In Katherine's absence, Molly had summoned Potter Ben and so he had to hear the story. Finally he said he would leave it up to Katherine but hoped she would wait to talk to Payton first. He offered to go hunt Payton and bring him back, but admitted their plan to travel three days into the mountains to the west. Ben even suggested that perhaps the captain of the Warsaw would wait, but as Carlton had explained, the repairs in Bermuda had put them months behind schedule and Carlton had begged for this extra day to look for Katherine; otherwise they would have sailed that morning. Leaving a sobbing Molly, a troubled Ben, and the Reverend asking God's blessings on the whole situation, Katherine and Jamie left Montgomery's Hundred with Carlton to set sail for England.

Chapter 13

At first Payton was angry and full of questions. Questions that were not answered in the letter Katherine had left him. Who was this man who had come and taken away his wife and his stepson? What did this man mean to Katherine? He must care a lot for her to come all this way at such expense. Molly had been able to add little to what the letter told him, except to say that the young man was a fine-looking man of good breeding. Potter Ben had little to add, and Reverend Swann reminded Payton that his stubborn refusal to admit his love for Katherine was the thing that would possibly keep her from ever returning. Swann suggested that if a few weeks without her showed Payton how blind he had been, it would be a good idea to let her know.

On top of the heartache and the fear, there were the embarrassing explanations at every turn. He had to deal with the parents of the school children and those who came at first to have letters written. News had spread to other plantations that Katherine would write letters and occasionally some besides their own tenants would come to have a letter written. Why did she start all this and leave him to account for her absence? The worst part was looking into the eyes of those who asked about her and seeing his own doubt that she would ever return reflected in their eyes also.

After the initial anger, Payton began to examine the issues that Katherine had brought up in the letter she left for him. He had been amazed to discover that the woman he married was an Arlington. What were the odds, he wondered, that she would come here through such a string of unusual circumstances, and find her nephew? They were too great to be random. He could only pray that the same forces that had brought her to him, would be with her and Jamie until justice was served. Payton had also begun to sense the depth of his feelings for Katherine. It was hard to imagine, that a woman raised in such wealth and high esteem, would develop such loving, unselfish qualities. She

99

had crept through the barriers he had set up and entrenched herself in his heart. Her very presence around the plantation had become a light to him and everyone around her. The people of the plantation had taken such pride in her, in the school she started, and in the hope she inspired in the children of Montgomery's Hundred. Some tenants were even talking of allowing their daughters to begin learning, so that as mothers they might provide the education unavailable to the children growing up in the remoteness of plantation life. In the short time she had been here she had helped them to see a vision of a country where equality was a possibility. Through the children she had begun a process to help them become aware of the equality of all God's children, including the Indians. She was teaching them that it is the responsibility of the individual to find that which is equal and worthy within themselves, and then to nourish it and encourage it into fruition. It was her belief that once we recognize our own equality, we begin to recognize it as the inherent right of all.

Payton had grown accustomed to her coming and going around the plantation. He now realized that he had unconsciously managed to place himself where he could catch a glimpse of her on and off during the day. He missed her sorely, the sight of her and the feel of her. He woke up at night hunting for her, chilled without the warmth of her body next to him. The passion that she had awakened within him demanded fulfillment at regular intervals, and he found himself as in the days of his youth making love to a fantasy and spilling his seeds into a handkerchief. He missed the special pains she took with his meals and the vegetables she had taught him to appreciate. The hours they had spent together after supper engaged in thought-provoking conversations were now the loneliest of the day. How could it be that he had not been more aware of the serenity and completeness she brought to his life? How could he have been so blind to the love that had grown steadily between them? In all the little ways that a woman shows her love for a man, Katherine had unashamedly expressed love for him. He had deceived

100

himself and her into believing himself above such emotions. As wrenching as his sense of loss, was the pain of regret for all that could have been.

Reverend Swann knew that Payton had loved Katherine from the beginning. Perhaps Payton didn't realize it himself, or it could be that his conception of love was too deeply tied to the fear of hurt. On the first Sunday of her absence he had spoken on love. Not love for the multitudes, but love for those who share our lives, those so close to us that we become blind to their need for love and assurance. He spoke of the need to give and accept love, reminding them that love is an integral part of the health and well-being of every heart that beats. "To renounce love is to renounce life," he said. From the Holy Scriptures he quoted the qualities of love, not so that each might see where they fell short, but so that they might cultivate and experience more of the giving, receiving nature of love.

Payton suspected the sermon was for him and wondered if the others thought that too. It didn't anger him for he was in pain. Obviously his belief that shielding oneself from love would shield one from pain was erroneous. Through the weeks that followed, he thought on this, considering the strangling effect it had on one, to cut oneself off from feeling. He weighed the value of a life lived in such a manner. He imagined the twisted results of children raised under such a belief. He realized that he had forced God to intervene, for his own good and for the good of those emotionally attached to him, now and in the future. If there was still to be a future for him. Mentally and spiritually he began the process of changing, calling a halt to his thinking when it slipped into old routes. Even if Katherine never returned, he knew he didn't want to go through his life afraid to love or be loved. She had opened a door that gave him a glimpse of something worth any risk.

By the time a ship came into Jamestowne, Payton was frantic to get word to her. He wanted first to dispel any doubts she might have concerning him and the death of her brother. He began by telling her how he had stopped by after Angela got

101

home from the play to tell her good-bye, for he was to sail to Virginia on the morn. They had a short visit where he brought her up to date on the welfare of her family and she told him of her secret marriage to Samuel Arlington. She had then told Payton that she believed she might be with child and was waiting a few more days on her menses before telling anyone. Samuel hadn't yet told his parents that they were wed, and she hoped the news of her pregnancy might give him the courage to tell them. She loved your brother very much, Katherine, she was willing to do whatever it took to make Samuel and your family proud of her. Angela walked me to the door and in a sisterly fashion I gave her a kiss and a hug. I turned and found your brother standing there drunk and angry. At the prodding of the man who was with him, he challenged me to a duel. Seeing that your brother was too drunk to be thinking straight, much less, shooting straight, I told him I would meet him at dawn in the park. When dawn came I was well out to sea.

Shortly after I arrived in Virginia, Angela showed up on another ship. She told me that Samuel had been taken home dead on the morning we were to duel. She had fled because she feared she would be blamed for his death and also feared for her life and that of her unborn child. Samuel had warned her not to tell Robbie of their marriage before he broke the news to his parents. Samuel feared that Robbie, as next in line, was becoming obsessed with the inheritance. Samuel's passion for Angela and his talk of marriage, had shown him a side of Robbie that seemed extremely threatened and desperate. Samuel had gone so far as to caution Angela not to open the door to Robbie, should he call upon her alone.

As soon as I heard of your brother's death, I wrote to your father and explained exactly what had happened. I told him that your cousin Robbie had been with your brother when last I saw him and suggested he make inquiries concerning Robbie since he had the most to gain from your brother's death. Angela was adamant that I tell your father nothing about the marriage or the child. As I now realize that your father's death came so swiftly

102

on the heels of my advice to him, I wonder about your father's death as well. I ask that you get Jamie proclaimed as heir as soon as possible and let no one know of his existence until you do. You must take every precaution. Do not underestimate your cousin; your own safety and Jamie's is at stake.

After stressing the danger of their situation to Katherine, Payton tried to find the words to let her know how much he missed her and wanted her to come back.

His first impulse had been to go after her in an effort to protect them and to let her know how much he loved her. He knew his chances of getting her back would be greater if he could confront her in person. Then he remembered how heavily his livelihood depended on the tobacco crop that must soon be planted and tended. The tobacco beds were set with seeds already germinating beneath their cover. There was no one whom he could leave with the responsibility of his crop. The very lives of the tenants and their families were dependent upon them getting their own crops planted. Even though the tenants were obligated to help him, the full burden of his, the largest crop by far, could not be carried by anyone but himself. Katherine and Jamie were truly more important than even his plantation here, but all the people of his 'hundred' were dependent on each other. If he lost what he had, they too would lose theirs. He could not risk that which was not his to risk. He tried as best he could to tell her in the letter that her absence had made him see that love for her had grown within him the whole time he was denying it. He wanted her to know how very much he needed her, but he also wanted to allow her to come back of her own free will. He told her how much the tenants missed her and that the school children kept asking if she would soon return. As he sealed the letter and made ready to send it by the ship now unloading goods at his dock, he realized how his interest and his ambition for Montgomery's Hundred had waned since Katherine's departure. His thoughts had begun to wander back to his home and family, and there was within him a need to restore love and peace to the relationships dearest to him. He pacified himself with a promise to go back as soon as this year's crop was hung to dry. He would find Katherine and if she was still his, he would take her to meet his father and brother. He would show her his homeland, and they would take the time to really get to know one another.

Chapter 14

The trip back to England was more comfortable than her trip to the colony. Carlton had been able to procure a cabin on the upper deck for Katherine and Jamie to share and one for himself next to it. Katherine used the weeks of travel to teach Jamie, not only basic education but history and stories of their family. Now that she knew him to be her nephew, she wanted him to know his grandfather, his grandmother, and his father. She hoped that through her stories they might become as real and alive to him as they had been to her. She promised to show him portraits of them once they were home and the business of his inheritance cleared away. Carlton also had stories to tell of Samuel, Jamie's father, and Katherine learned much about her brother that she had not known. They could only hope that what they were saying and teaching him was getting through to him. Jamie's eyes were ever aware and alert now and though he never spoke, he communicated through facial expressions and had begun more and more to use his hands to motion for things he wanted. Katherine sensed that there was a quick intelligence there, and through his art and penmanship she could see that he was learning the education basics.

She and Carlton also had time for long talks and the more they pondered Samuel's death and that of her father, the more they realized the danger they were taking Jamie into. Katherine planned to take Jamie to the small house left to her by her great aunt Katherine. She hoped that Barrister Dunbar had been able to get it cleaned and repaired by now. If her servants had taken up residence there, that would be even more convenient. She needed people around Jamie whom she could trust, people who would be genuinely concerned for his welfare.

Katherine missed Payton from the moment she set sail. Every knot took her farther away from him. In her heart she never doubted that he was her destiny and that they would be together again. A part of her wished fervently that he would come after her. Fantasies played out in her head of him coming and declaring his love for her. She indulged in scenes of their lovemaking, of the two of them enjoying the wonderful sights and sounds of London together, of him taking her to Langley to meet his family and sharing his childhood with her. She wanted to meet Jamie's maternal grandparents. She thought it might help ease the pain of their daughter's death to know that Angela had left them something of herself. Another part of Katherine was glad for this time alone to take care of her affairs independently. Too many things in her life, in her mind, in her emotions, and in her affairs had been left in a state of fragmentation. She welcomed this time to sort through and clear the clutter away so that she could embrace the present and all it had to offer.

By the time they reached England she and Carlton had become close friends and business partners. He had shared with her the state of his affairs as left to him by his father, and they realized the mutual benefits of having him take over management of the shipping firm. She wasn't sure how their discovery of Jamie would affect her ownership of that firm. Carlton told her that Mr. Barlow had said it was to go to her and then to her first-born. She reasoned that if she and Carlton together could come up with enough money to get it back in business, and he took over the management, they could share any profits that Carlton made for them. All of which would have to be worked out with Barrister Dunbar.

The sight of their homeland was a joy to everyone on the ship, and Katherine watched the amazement in Jamie's eyes as they were helped from the small boats into a world he had never experienced. Carlton hired a carriage to carry them to his house in Whitehall. Upon entering, Jamie seemed to withdraw into himself, almost as if overwhelmed by the magnificence of this totally unfamiliar world. After the joyous greetings of Carlton's staff, who were relieved to have him home and safe, Carlton introduced Katherine and Jamie simply by their first names. He said they were friends who made the trip back with him and would need a room to use until their own home was made ready for them. Katherine could sense their curiosity and felt again the immediacy with which they must get Jamie established as heir. She took Jamie's hand and together they followed Carlton's housekeeper to a room that adjoined what appeared to have been a nursery.

"The child seems scared, Miss. 'Twould be easier on him to be near his Ma if ye think this suitable."

"Thank you, Jane, this is perfect." Katherine could see that Jane was anxious to stay and find out more about the two of them and their connection with Carlton. Jane insisted on helping them get settled, while keeping up a steady stream of leading questions. Katherine finally thanked her again and told her she would like to be alone with Jamie. Once alone with him she tried to put him at ease with the new surroundings. She explained that Jamestowne and the plantations of Virginia were newly established. "London and the towns on this side of the ocean have been developing for hundreds of years," she told him.

"One day, when enough builders and craftsmen settle in Virginia, it too will have streets with tall buildings that house fine furnishings. You will soon become used to all this and instead of being fearful you will marvel at the wonders of man's ingenuity. You will give thanks for and enjoy the conveniences of refinement. Because you have experienced life without them, you will not take all this for granted, and you will be a better man for it." With that she ruffled his hair and told him that this was probably the room that Carlton used when he was a little boy. She then assured him that the door between their rooms would be left open. Together they went back into her room and removing their shoes they lay together on her bed to rest. Carlton would return soon with news of her house and servants. The sooner they could leave from here the sooner the servants would forget they were ever here.

Carlton went to the smallhouse where Samuel and Katherine's grandfather and grandmother Randolph had lived when in London. Their grandfather had left it to his sister, who

107

had outlived him by several years. She died, leaving the house to Katherine.

Roberta answered the door and anxiously gathered the others at Carlton's request that all be present. Roberta, a failing Arthur and Cooke Della stood before him braced for bad news. Maggie had taken employment with the family her husband worked for upon dismissal by Robbie.

Carlton first asked if they were the only one's living there before he began. "I have brought Katherine home. She is now at my house in Whitehall awaiting word of circumstances here." Relief spread over their faces, followed by tears. They sensed there was more and stood quietly. "Before I continue, I must swear you all to secrecy for it is a matter of life and death."

Roberta, put out by the insult, spoke for the three of them. "Sir, we have been loyal to the Arlingtons for all our working years. Especially now, at our age, any danger to them is a danger to us. Quit yer beating around the bush and tell us what has happened to Lady Katherine. We have been worried sick and will not stand here another minute swearing to a loyalty that has been proven time and again."

"As soon as I can fetch her from my house at Whitehall, I will be bringing Katherine here with Samuel Arlington's young son." At their rush of questions, he held up his hand for silence." 'Tis a long story and I will leave the details to Katherine. The boy is alive because it was known to no one on this side of the ocean that he exists. He is heir to the fortune that most likely got his father killed. Every precaution must be taken to assure his safety until the matter of his inheritance is straightened out and Cousin Robbie has nothing to gain by harming him. Katherine has the greatest trust in you and I know that neither of you would knowingly break that trust. 'Tis the unthinking slip or loving indulgence that worries me most. The boy is a mirror image of Samuel at that age, and anyone who knew the father would recognize the child. For his grandfather Matthew, his father Samuel and for the child, Jamie, I beg you to be ever mindful of what is said and what is seen concerning this child. I leave it in

108

your hands to trust your own wisdom even above that of Katherine, for there are dangers that she may not see. Now I go to bring them here, for my own servants are not as trustworthy as you."

With one excited speculation after another, the servants passed the time until the carriage returned. The child, wrapped in a blanket, was carried in by Carlton amidst the joyful reunion of Katherine and those who were as family to her. Carlton removed the blanket to reveal a startled Jamie surrounded by strangers acting as if they knew him. They could barely restrain themselves from reaching out and grabbing him.

"Aw, 'tis the child Samuel made over," Roberta sobbed. 'Twas the last dream of ye father, Miss, and he died with a broken heart, never to know that his fondest wish had already been granted."

"Perhaps my father is looking down on us now, admiring his fine grandson. It gives me comfort to think so Roberta. Now that I am married and with child myself, I would thank you not to refer to me as Miss," Katherine added in a joking manner. She took a moment to enjoy the shocked look on all their faces and then went on, "That's a story that can wait, for now we must get Jamie acquainted with his new family." Katherine introduced the boy to each one of them, telling him of times in her and her brother's childhood when the one being introduced had come to the rescue of a child in danger of being wrongfully punished or had gotten them out of a jam of some sort.

Jamie took an immediate liking to Arthur. He eased up to him and kept pointing to his eyes. When they couldn't understand, Jamie pulled at his own eyebrows and then Katherine knew. Arthur had great bushy eyebrows and Jamie wanted to touch them, for he had never seen any like them. Arthur took him upon his knee and let him touch the long hairs, that curled out from his brows. Tears ran down the old mans cheeks as the child gently examined the brows with his fingers. "'Twas ever a bemusement to ye father too that my eyebrows were like a brushpile. Ye father used to like to ride my horse

109

too." With that he took Jamie's hands and in spite of the rheumatism that had settled there, he gave the boy a ride, clicking his tongue to the motion of his knee. Jamie gave the old man one of his rare smiles and allowed Arthur to hug him close for a moment. Roberta and Cooke, now jealous that the boy had accepted Arthur first, plied for his attention. Cooke with sweetbread and Roberta with a box of toys she had found and moved from the big house. The three of them soon realized that Jamie had not made a sound, and as soon as he was fed and put down for the night, Katherine answered all their questions.

It was aboard the Warsaw that Katherine had realized she was pregnant. At first she had thought the morning sickness to be seasickness, but when her menses never came, she knew she was with child. Today had been her very first mention of it. Even Carlton had been shocked. Arthur, himself from the north, knew of Payton's family and their influence there. He felt that she had married well in spite of Payton being a second son. It showed on the faces of Roberta and Cooke that they were not so sure. They could only hope that Katherine's faith in Payton was justly placed and that he truly had no part in the death of Samuel.

Carlton came the next morning to take Katherine to the office of Barrister Dunbar. They wanted to talk to him about the legalities they faced with the shipping business, Katherine's inheritance, and where they should begin in the process of claiming Jamie's inheritance. Jamie was by now comfortable with the servants; in fact, he had them wrapped around his finger. Katherine explained that she and Carlton were going to take care of some business and left him happily going through the big box of toys from the nursery of her youth.

Arnold Dunbar was a man of knowledge and integrity, who stayed informed on political, ecclesiastical, and economic affairs. He was ever astute in applying this knowledge to the affairs of his clients and his friends. Katherine's father Matthew had been friend and client. Upon hearing of Jamie, his face broke into a frown and he sat behind it in thought for a moment. "We are indeed fortunate that Payton Montgomery has been declared the

110

legal guardian of Samuel's child and that he is a gentleman whose family is in favor with the king," he said. "This would be a bad time to bring forth a minor child who is heir to a fortune without a declared guardian of good standing. King James, in his greed and desperate financial state, has discovered an old feudal law that allows the king to appoint a guardian for a minor child left by any man of means. Through this practice he has been able to skim off the immediate funds, leaving the guardian to the unscrupulous use of the child and all that is left of his estate. You see, King James has not the power to raise taxes; Parliament must approve any tax increases. Parliament continues to use this power to bargain with the King, alas, to no avail. They have a list of grievances for which they demand attention each time Parliament is called, and each time they meet it ends in a stalemate. The power to call Parliament is left to the king. He can go for years without calling them if it so pleases His Majesty. We have a king who would drain our country if not for Parliament. He came here from a poor country, believing this to be a very rich country with unlimited funds. His obsession for comely young males has cost us dearly, not to mention the other extremes to which his extravagance is noted. He is ever looking for ways to gain income without having to pacify the demands of Parliament. I feel confident that the king will not interfere in this case. It would not be worth losing the support that he holds in the north. I would advise you to get everything in order so that when the time is right we can move quickly. Obtain the Certificate of Marriage as soon as possible and get it to me; that plus this Certificate of Birth which names Jamie an Arlington and the sworn statement of Payton Montgomery as to guardianship, should be adequate proof. The child's resemblance to Samuel will further enhance the factual material. I will draw up the necessary papers to release the funds from your trust and a contract allowing Carlton to manage the shipping firm for you at the percentage of profits agreed upon. It is possible that Payton Montgomery could object to any of this and win. I believe that even though you used a false name, his

111

marriage to you would stand in court. Do you feel that he would disagree with any of the decisions you have made, Katherine?"

"No, sir, he has never been unduly concerned where dowry or anything material is concerned. He respects my opinion and would, I believe, respect my decisions concerning my own inheritance. His mother was allowed to control her inheritance. She used it for Payton's schooling and left the remainder to him as second son."

Chapter 15

The first few days in London were spent getting a routine set for Katherine and Jamie. Because of all the changes that Jamie had recently gone through, Katherine felt it important to Jamie's healing that they give him the security of routine.

Keeping much to themselves and taking every precaution to insure the safety of the child took priority over the many things Katherine was anxious to do. Because the smallhouse was tightly crowded into a space between others like it, an enclosed garden in back gave the family a measure of outdoor privacy. Jamie was allowed to play there when weather permitted. Inside, Katherine kept him occupied a good deal of the time with books and learning. She was delighted with all that London could provide in the way of children's books and instructional material, along with toys that taught and amused. Carlton found a children's doctor and after a through examination by Dr. Martin, Jamie was found to be in good health. The only explanation for his muteness seemed to be the trauma he suffered as witness to the death of his mother and sister. Dr. Martin suggested that Katherine hire a girl named Susan Wiley to come and work with Jamie. Susan's younger sister had been raped at a young age and had reacted very much like Jamie. Susan had learned everything she could about this malady and now worked as a nurse to children with trauma-related illness. Dr. Martin would contact her and see if she could arrange to take Jamie's case anytime soon. Before the week was out Susan Wiley came to meet Jamie and see if she thought she might be able to help him. Susan was a beautiful, dark-haired girl of Welsh descent as Jamie's mother had been, and Jamie warmed quickly to her loving nature. After an hour or so with him she and Katherine talked in private.

"Lady Montgomery, it appears to me that someone has been doing the right things, and Jamie has become very aware for a child with this problem. I feel hopeful that he could reach full recovery within a shorter time than most of the patients I see. It

pleases me that he has learned so many educational skills. Too
often people think that because the child doesn't speak that he
will not comprehend. I would like to begin next Tuesday to
spend two hours with him twice a week. As soon as I have a
shift in my schedule I will perhaps add more time. I am anxious
to get started with Jamie. He is the type of child who makes my
work fulfilling, and I appreciate this opportunity to further my
studies and my theories on these types of illnesses."

Katherine was impressed with Susan and felt she would like
to know her better. There were few women whom Katherine
could relate to with the intimacy of a good friend, and she
thought Susan might be such a woman. More than that she was
pleased with Susan's attitude in regard to Jamie and her work.
"Miss Wiley, I know Jamie and I are fortunate in finding
someone of your ability and apparent knowledge. Please arrange
your schedule to include as much time with Jamie as possible,
and with your instructions I will follow through when you are
not here. There is, however, one thing I must ask of you. It is
important that no one know of Jamie's existence at this time. His
very life may depend on that. My instincts tell me you are a
person who can be trusted, and I will explain this to you in more
detail when I know you better. For right now, will you agree to
keep this whole matter confidential and in no way let it be
known that a small boy lives here, mentioning his name to no
one?"

"Lady Montgomery, I admit that you have aroused my
curiosity, but I also sense that this is more than an irrational fear
on your part. You can trust me to keep this to myself for as long
as this child is in danger, with or without further explanation."

They then discussed fees, and when Susan left Katherine
was thankful that Susan had been referred to them and thankful
that through her father she now had the funds to pay for such
services.

Carlton stopped by later and Katherine excitedly told him of
Susan's evaluation of Jamie and of her agreement to keep their
secret. Carlton was not so comfortable with this news and said

he would like to meet the woman when she came on Tuesday. In the meantime he would check out her references.

The next morning Katherine dressed for her meeting with Robbie. The day after her return home she had sent a messenger to ask that he meet with her as soon as possible. He had sent word that she could visit at any time but that he would not be available to see her until today. Katherine wanted to see her mother and she had an idea about getting Samuel's old carriage and the marriage certificate. As she was let into what used to be her home, she was glad to see that Robbie had made some tasteful improvements.

Robbie, with new confidence and fashionable attire, came from the library to greet Katherine. Even though he grasped her hand and gave her a hug, there was a restraint that clearly showed he was afraid she had come begging. He took her into the library, making small talk until she was seated there, then looked askance.

"First of all I would like to know how Mother is doing and thank you for letting her stay here."

"Katherine, your mother is not here. I have had her moved to a sanatorium in Dartfoorde. A Dr. Sanford who is doing some experiments in addictions and emotional problems was called in by Mother when she saw the state of Marie's health. She wasn't eating or even conscious most of the time. Mother feared for her life. We tried to handle it ourselves at first, but Mr. Barlow and your servants were unable to refuse her the laudanum. After I asked Mr. Barlow to leave and dismissed your servants, your mother sank into melancholy. Mother heard some good things of this Dr. Sanford and contacted him. He insisted on taking her to his sanatorium where he could monitor her care. He uses herbs and a special diet to strengthen her body and ease her craving of laudanum. He says that his patients become mentally stronger by being away from everything that may contribute to the cause of their addiction. Mother says it is a lovely place where patients are well-treated. There are beautiful gardens and patients are required to spend some time each day, weather

115

permitting, in nature. They are also required to spend time with other patients, Dr. Sanford's theory being that nature and learning to care about others helps to restore mind and body."

"I am thankful that Aunt Rachel was able to find such a doctor. I too feared for Mother's life. Please tell her how much I appreciate what she has done for my mother. How long will Mother be required to stay at this institution? Will I be able to visit her there or write to her?"

"In about two weeks, your mother will be allowed to receive visitors. Any written communication must be short and of a positive nature, making no reference to family problems. As to the length of time she must stay there, it is dependent on how well she responds to treatment. This treatment is expensive and her monthly allowance from your father barely covers the treatment. I suggest you inquire as to any personal needs she might have and provide for them. Is there anything else that you wished to discuss with me?"

"Robbie as you have probably heard I am living in the smallhouse that Aunt Katherine wanted me to have after her death. I am very comfortable there but I find myself without transportation. I have come to ask if you might part with Samuel's buggy. Space is so limited there I only have room to keep something small. For the short trips I make, the buggy would be adequate. Of course I would be willing to pay you for it. The sentimental value to me is worth more than the monetary value. I see all these newly designed vehicles around town and think how Samuel was ever the leader in what he called wheels. His must look sadly outdated beside the newer ones, which matters little to me, not like it would to a man of your taste. You have done wonderful things to the house and you look so well put together. I am glad to see someone with pride taking over. Mr. Barlow really let the place go down. I also want you to know I appreciate you letting my servants take the personal things of my family and especially the pictures, those things are so dear to me and will be to my children one day."

Robbie had sat concentrating on her every word as if looking for any hidden meaning. He had been that way as a young boy, ever fearful that someone might pull something over on him. Now, after a short silence, he seemed to make a decision and bring his attention to Katherine. "I hear you are now wed to some chap in the colony, is that so?" He was his usual blunt self. "What's it like over there, disgusting and uncivilized is what I hear."

"Yes I am married to Payton Montgomery, I'm sure you've heard of the Northumberland Montgomerys. Payton has a plantation on the James River. Since we have our own community there and produce everything we need, I see little of the colony as a whole. To me it is much like being at our country estate. Remember how we used to go there for the summer and have such good times? Of course, there are not yet the grand manors and permanent structures of our countryside, but Payton's home is quite comfortable.

"How long will you be in London?" he asked.

"I'm not sure," Katherine answered. "There was the business of my trust to be taken care of and the shipping firm that became bankrupt under Mr. Barlow. I am putting some money back into it, and Carlton Edwards is going to take over the management of that for me. Of course I will have to make a trip north to Langley and get acquainted with my new family. It could be such a long time before I get back to London, I intend to enjoy some of the things I have missed. Right now, Payton is busy getting the tobacco crops planted and though I miss him desperately, it will be harvest before he has much time for me."

"Send Arthur around for the buggy. I have no use for it," Robbie said as if in dismissal. "My Mother is down in Brighton to visit her sister. She will want to call on you before you leave, as she worried so about you when you disappeared."

"Of course, tell Aunt Rachel to let me know so that I can arrange a nice visit. I've been rushing out so much on business matters, I wouldn't want to miss her. Now if you will tell me a price, I will be glad to pay for the buggy." When Robbie waved

117

her out as if to say, take it, it's nothing, Katherine thanked him and let herself out. She sent Arthur back by the carriage she had hired and within an hour she had Samuel's certificate of marriage in her hand.

During her visit with Robbie she had surprised her own self with the suggestion of going to Langley. Now as she pondered that unconscious desire, she thought it a good idea. She would like to know more about Payton's family, and she would like Jamie to know his grandparents there. If she decided to return to the colony, it would comfort her to know they were available to visit with him and show him love. When she mentioned it to Carlton he suggested that the weather made such a trip miserable at this time of year. Mid-April or May would be so much more enjoyable and by then he could arrange for them to sail up the coast and take a coach from the closest point. Sailing would eliminate much of the travel on rough, washed-out roads, and cut the travel time in half or more. Katherine was thrilled with that idea and looked forward to such a trip with excitement. As soon as she had talked to Barrister Dunbar, she had written a letter to Payton telling him of the progress they had made so far in establishing Jamie as heir. At the beginning, she was very business like and cool. Then as she pictured him reading it, she weakened, her heart reaching out to him with sudden longing. "I love you Payton and I always shall. I realize that you have probably not had time or opportunity to get any word to me. I have, as yet, come to no conclusion about our future. I can only hope that when I do hear from you there will be an honest expression of your feelings for me, something to weigh against the desirable qualities of living in my homeland."

Carlton had found a ship departing for the colony and sent the letter the very next day.

Susan had been coming for two weeks and Jamie had grown so fond of her that he cooperated in all the little exercises she put him through. She was careful not to ask him to do things he was not yet ready to try. There were several things that Susan asked Jamie to do on his own when no one was around. Katherine wished she had thought of such things, for she could see where they might lead. Susan would recite a little nursery rhyme and then tell Jamie to practice it when he was alone so that some day when he began talking again he would be able to recite it for her. Susan had the wonderful attitude of accepting that Jamie did not speak but assuring him that one day he would begin talking and they would have to gag him to get him to shut up. She suggested to him that he should sneak and try out his voice every once in a while, just to see if he still had one. Jamie and Katherine were not the only ones who had grown fond of Susan and admired her. Carlton had become obviously enamored of her and Katherine thought there might be some reciprocation on Susan's part. Carlton was like an older brother to Katherine and nothing would please her more than to see him happily in love with a woman of Susan's character.

When the letter arrived from Payton, it threw Katherine into an emotional upheaval. It was a four-page letter expressing, sometimes between the lines, his hurt, his anger, his fear, and most importantly, his love. His explanation of the confrontation with Samuel and of Payton's communication with her father after Samuel's death left her shocked and disturbed. Mingled in with a renewed fear of Robbie, was shock and anger that Robbie would go to such lengths to obtain wealth and power. Her father had treated Robbie like his own son. He had given to Robbie all that a man would normally give to a second son: education, a generous allowance, travels abroad. On several occasions he had picked up notes that Robbie was unable to pay, and though the details were kept from her, there were at least three times that she remembered when her father had been summoned to get Robbie out of serious trouble. In spite of Robbie's insolent attitude toward her father, he had always accepted responsibility for the boy. Samuel had been, from the time he was a child, a lovable and loving person. He accepted everyone, including Robbie, as they were. He was quick to forgive and willing to share anything he owned. She thought of the many times Samuel had stood up for Robbie and had helped him to become

119

accepted where he would never have been accepted, not because of family or position, as Robbie always thought, but because he was a person whom no one cared to be around. Samuel had enough popularity to carry Robbie and Robbie ever played that advantage. Katherine thought she had moved past the devastation of their deaths, but it all boiled up within her again. If Robbie was indeed responsible for the death of her brother and her father, he was indirectly to blame for all that her mother had gone through. She would seek the truth of this matter and she would find it. She was the only one left, she had to do it.

At that moment she thought of Reverend Swan and his messages to them on vengeance. No, she would not be driven by fear and anger. She would work on her feelings toward Robbie and from a higher level of thinking, she would trust a power greater than human to bring about the justice and closure necessary for healing to begin. Healing for herself, Jamie and her mother.

Chapter 16

I, Chanco, had been living with the Pace family at their plantation on the James River for two winters. We were moving into my second spring with them when my half-brother, Rawbunt, came with a message from Chief Opechancanough. A message that I was to rise before the Pace family awoke the next morning and stab Master Pace in his bed with a knife from the kitchen. I was then to take the guns from the house and deliver them to warriors who would be waiting just out of sight, upriver. I told Rawbunt that I had grown to love the Pace family and I did not think I could do this. He laughed at me and told me I had no choice. He said that by midday tomorrow all of the English would be wiped from the land of the Powhatans. With heavy heart I returned to my job of helping Mary Pace cut the seed potatoes.

Before I came to live with the Pace family, I had not known of potatoes. The Pace family would dig the potatoes in late summer and put them in a deep hole dug back into a little hill near the house. In the cool dark hole, the potatoes and other root vegetables would keep through the winter, providing food for the family. Even if the winter was hard and food was scarce, some potatoes were saved to start a new crop. By spring the potatoes would start to become shriveled and have green sprouts starting to grow from little indentations called eyes. Mary and I were to cut the shriveled potatoes so that each chunk had an eye from which a plant would grow when placed in the ground. By summer's end the plants would become wilted and dry. In the ground beneath the wilted plants we would dig and find a nest of potatoes. I liked them best when Mama Pace roasted them in the coals and ashes of the fire, and we ate them with fresh churned butter and bread still warm from the clay oven out back. Potatoes were just one of the good things I had learned about from living with the Pace family.

Tomorrow was a day the English called Good Friday. It was their custom to plant the early vegetables on that day. There was nothing for me to do but act as if the potatoes and the other vegetables would get planted; in my heart, I knew they would not.

"Chanco, what is wrong with you? You are leaving two eyes in some of these potatoes and none in others," Mary said.

"Ever since that hateful Rawbunt came with a message from your people, you have been in a stupor."

I looked up into Mary's blue eyes to see if she was angry with me. I saw not anger but concern. I then put my head back down so that she would not see my sadness. Mary accepted my silence with patience. She was the prettiest, most kindhearted girl I had ever known. Her hair glowed with the warmth and beauty of flames, orange and yellow. When I had first come here I could not resist the urge to touch Mary's flaming hair. She had seemed to understand my fascination and sometimes allowed me to brush her hair after supper when we sat on the porch. Mary brought forth from my heart a warm, tender feeling that I could not hide. She was older than me and had her cap set for a young Englishman who lived on another plantation. Still I could not help loving her and bringing her presents of wild flowers and things I found in nature. The Pace boys teased me, making up jokes and songs about us, but they meant no harm.

My sadness hung like a black cloud over me the rest of the afternoon. I feared greatly the threat of an attack on this family. I feared also the war that would follow and its effect on my people. Mary and I had reached the bottom of the basket, and I was grateful she had allowed me my silence. Andrew, James, and Timothy Pace had come in from preparing the garden for planting. Mary told me to go play for a while before the evening chores. I helped her carry the cut seed potatoes and our utensils to the back porch. Then I went down to the dock by the river. I sat there in silence, hoping that the voices of the Ancient Ones would come to me in the wind or the waters and tell me what I should do.

122

*   *   *

During the evening of a beautiful spring day in March, Payton rowed home from Jamestowne. The next day was Good Friday, the day they would begin planting the early food crops. He had gone into town to take care of some business and to purchase additional seed for planting on the morrow. A chance meeting with Governor Wyatt as he was ready to leave had resulted in him getting a late start home. Governor Wyatt had wanted to tell him of an incident that had happened several weeks back with Chief Opechancanough.

It was said that Opechancanough had few of the leadership qualities of his brother, Powhatan. He hated all whites because of some prior experience with the Spanish. His ego was such that he felt threatened by any one of his own race who gained favor with his people. He had a rival named Nemattanow, a man lovingly called, "Jack o' the Feather," by the Indians, a name he had earned for his agility of mind and body in a fight. Nemattanow was the Powhatans hero warrior. The Powhatans believed, and Nemattanow agreed, that he was indestructible. Nemattanow loved to do what he was best at and was ever instigating trouble with the whites. Opechancanough, thinking to rid himself of his rival and incite the anger of his people against the English, had a few months before sent word to Governor Wyatt that Wyatt had the chief's permission to cut Nemattanow's throat. Governor Wyatt dismissed the message as something personal between the two of them and was disturbed when, in an affray with two settlers, Nemattanow was shot and killed. Opechancanough immediately became grief-stricken and came before the governor dressed in all his chieftain plumage, haughtily demanding ridiculous concessions for his incensed people. When his demands were refused Opechancanough flew into a rage, uttering curses upon the English. The governor and his secretary became startled at this display of savage fury and called in the guard. Opechancanough immediately calmed down and begged their pardon. He then became humble, declaring his

123

love for the friends of former Chief Powhatan's family. "Sooner will the skies fall than my bond of friendship be dissolved," he had said in parting. Opechancanough had done an about-face so quickly that the governor had become worried that he was up to some treachery. Wyatt had mentioned his fear around town, but no one had seemed concerned at that time. Now rumors had reached him that Opechancanough had been holding secret meetings with the chiefs of other tribes. The Governor wanted Payton's assessment of this situation.

Payton had told the governor it wouldn't hurt to make the people aware that the Indians were still angry over the death of Nemattanow and that there could be trouble. "I will warn those along the river on my way home, tell them to watch for any unusual activity among the Indians. Perhaps you should send messengers to those up the river toward the falls."

"Aye, I will see to it at the beginning of next week," Wyatt had told Payton.

As Payton neared the dock of Pace's Pains, he saw Chanco, the smaller of the two Indian boys who lived with Richard, sitting on the dock with head down as if in deep thought. As Payton approached, the boy stood to give him a hand and to tie the canoe.

"Lady Montgomery, she no come back yet?" Chanco asked.

"No, Chanco, I haven't heard from her, so I don't know when to expect her back. I stopped to speak to Richard, is he home?"

"No, sir, he go see Mrs. Proctor and help her make sick cow better. Andrew here, you talk to him maybe?"

"Perhaps I will talk to Mrs. Pace. Is she at the house?"

"Yes, sir, may I ask you question first, you wise man, you tell Chanco, must Chanco do what he is told even when heart say that very bad thing to do?"

"Chanco, as a grown man I would listen to my heart. You, as a child, must decide if the person who gave you the order, is trustworthy and has your best interests at heart."

Payton didn't want to alarm Mrs. Pace but felt it necessary to caution them. He told her that the Indians were angry over the recent shooting of Nemattanow and Chief Opechancanough could be using the incident to stir up other tribes and gain their support. Mrs. Pace said she was getting ready to send James over to Mrs. Proctor's to stay the night with her and help with the birth of a calf. 'Twas the heifer's first and it had been having some problems. Mrs. Proctor was a widow with children to feed, and the cow was an important source of food for them. She would have James warn Mrs. Proctor. Richard would come home when James got there to relieve him and they would make some preparations just in case. She gave Payton a fresh deer ham and told him how much the boys missed Lady Montgomery and the school.

After Mr. Montgomery left, I went to help with the evening chores, getting in wood and water and seeing to the animals. I knew that Mr. Montgomery had taken my question seriously and had given me the best answer he could, I just didn't know if such an answer would apply to this situation. If Lady Montgomery were here I could speak freely with her. She cared about all people and would not want anyone to get hurt. I did not know her husband so well. Once when I had told her that I was one with the Great Spirit, she had told me that all were one with the same Spirit. There is one Creator who answers to many names, she had said. Even though I needed her now, I was glad that she would not be here on the morrow. Perhaps the Great Spirit had saved her by sending her away.

During supper the Pace family were absorbed in discussing the Easter ceremony that was to take place on Sunday in Jamestowne. I was glad they didn't notice my silence and my lack of appetite. When dusk came I felt none of the peace and contentment I usually felt. Evening had always been a special time at the Pace home. When all the chores were done, supper over, and the big metal dishpans hung back on their pegs after the washing, scalding, and drying of the supper utensils, all the family came together. When weather permitted we gathered on the porch to sit in quiet contemplation or visit with tenants of the plantation who would stop by with stories and news. Sometimes there would be music and songs, or we children would play games until bedtime. During cold weather, we gathered around the fire in the main hall. Master Pace told us stories of long ago in England when people came from other lands to plunder and take from the English. Once he looked at me and said he was ashamed of those English who had learned nothing from the stories of their own past. That's when I told him that I was born to be the storyteller of my grandmother's people, so that I might keep alive the wisdom of the Ancient Ones. When I was three months in the womb of my mother, my grandmother had begun to tell me the stories and sing me the songs of the Ancient Ones. My first six years of life had been given to learning the songs, stories, and ceremonies of the Ancient Ones. My grandmother was of the Wisdom Keepers and I had been chosen to take her place when her spirit left her body. Often Master Pace would read to us from a book called the Bible. When he read to us the stories from the Bible I could see what Lady Montgomery meant; even though we called our Creator by different names and the stories were told in different words, the messages were the same. They were messages of love and honor, for our Creator, ourselves and all others.

Although today had been sunny and warm, the setting sun had taken its warmth with it, and the family sat inside by the fire. Mary and her mother were sewing on the new dresses they planned to wear on Easter. It seemed as if everything that was said and done after Rawbunt's visit reminded me that this family might not be alive after tomorrow morning.

Payton rowed on past his dock to warn Ralph Hamor. By this time dark was no more than an hour or two away and there were preparations to take care of at his hundred. It could be days, even weeks before they retaliated, if they did. Payton worried most about the newcomers to the colony. The Powhatans were devious enemies, pretending to be friends right up to the last minute. In making a round to warn his tenants, Payton discovered that three of Opechancanough's men had come visiting earlier that evening. They had brought fish and had stayed to eat and drink with the Robinson family; they were camped nearby. They had told Mrs. Robinson to have the pan on the fire at daybreak for they had spotted a covey of quail and would move like foxes upon them before they came off the roost. When Payton tried to make the Robinsons realize there might be danger he could see that they thought him overly concerned. Potter Ben, intent upon warning friends at Martin's Hundred and the Bennett plantation, left by moonlight in a canoe. Payton warned each household on the place to get women and children into the stockade at the first sign of anything suspicious. He and some of the men wet down as best they could the food storage buildings. They filled every container they could find with water and placed them in the stockade.

When Mama Pace said it was bedtime, young Timothy put up his usual fight against wearing the white flannel gown. Every night during cold weather, Mama Pace insisted that Timothy take off his knee britches, wash up, and put on the gown. Every night Timothy resisted. Last winter, I too had been required to sleep in a warm gown, for Mama Pace said that she had promised to take care of me as if I were her own child. I too hated the gown and felt as if I were tied up in a sack all night. I was thankful that Mama Pace had considered me too old for the gown this winter. As usual, Mama Pace won the fight with Timothy, also the fight to tuck Timothy in and kiss him goodnight.

On the way to our loft bed, I picked up Timothy's britches from the floor where he had left them. "What do you carry in your pockets that is so heavy?" I asked the boy after Mama Pace had gone down the steps.

"Just stuff," Timothy had answered.

"Probably some of my stuff," Andrew said. "Let me see." Andrew was the oldest of the Pace children. When Master Pace was not around, Andrew was in charge. He was usually fair and did not ask anything of us without good reason. He started

127

pulling items from the pockets: a flint, a small kitchen knife, a biscuit, toasted corn, dried venison, a slingshot and pebbles.

"Timothy, why do you have all this stuff in your pockets? Mama has been looking everywhere for this knife."

"Just do," Timothy answered. "I don't have to tell you, 'tis none of your business."

Andrew jumped up and grabbed Timothy by the hair. "You can tell me or I will call Father. Are you planning to run away or something?"

"No, let go of my hair, it's just some stuff I thought I might need. In case there should be an Indian attack or the Spanish should come up river. What if I got separated from everyone and had to hide out?"

Andrew softened, and letting go of Timothy's hair, he put his arm around the boy and hugged him. "I did that once myself, carried around everything I thought I might need if I got lost or fell in a deep hole or something. But ye need not worry lad. When Pocahontas married John Rolfe, Chief Powhatan declared that the Indians and the English were family and would live together in peace. Don't you remember the story?"

"Yeah, but Pocahontas is dead now and so is Chief Powhatan. His stepbrother, I can't say his name, is chief now and he's mad at all of us. Mr. Montgomery told Mama that the Indians were riled up over the shooting of their great warrior Jack o' the Feather. Two colonists shot the warrior. They're saying the Indian killed one of their friends and was wearing his hat. How about the Spanish? You don't know when they might decide to move north and attack us."

"If the Spanish should start up the river we would know and have plenty of time to get prepared," Andrew told him. "One shipload of Spanish would be no match for us, now that our colony has grown. I will take care of you, lad. Between the good Lord above and me right here, you don't have to be afraid. Besides, we've got Chanco. He is our brother. He would see that those Indians didn't hurt us, wouldn't you, Chanco?"

"If I could," I answered, and my heart felt as if it would break. After the light was blown out, I lay there sleepless. Fear and heartache were like huge stones in my chest. I could hardly breath. Finally, when I sensed that all were asleep, I slipped quietly down the steps and out the front door. I needed to be out under the stars. From the porch I saw Grandmother Moon and remembered the legends of my mother's people and the times they had called upon her for guidance.

"Grandmother Moon, it is I, Chanco, born of the Wisdom Keepers. I have been raised to be a storyteller. Taught to hear the voices of the Ancient Ones in the wind when it whispers through the pines and in the waters rushing to the sea. Born that I might tell their stories and share their wisdom with the generations to come. I do not have the heart to kill Master Pace and steal the guns that might save the others. If this is what you would have me do, then you must tear out my storyteller heart and replace it with the heart of a warrior."

Grandmother Moon began speaking to me without words. "Chanco, step out of the shadow and let me see you. My how you have grown. Sit there in that patch of light and let me think a moment. Oh yes, I remember your story now. Your grandmother's people were a peaceful tribe. They were captured by the Powhatans when your mother was just a baby. Your mother and grandmother have taught you to carry on the legends of your mother's people. What they have taught you is good, Chanco, and I would not tear it from your heart."

"But today, while you were sleeping Grandmother Moon, the Powhatans have gone to the English colonists as friends. At daybreak they will attack them in their homes, just as they did my mother's people. I have grown to love the English family I live with, but I also love my father and his people, the Powhatans. I have been ordered to stab Master Pace and take his guns, leaving the Pace family helpless against our warriors when morning comes. I do not think I can do this thing, yet I do not want to shame my father or cause my own people to die."

"Chanco, you have been raised according to truths that were given to all mankind. Truths that somehow get twisted according to the whims of man. The Ancient Ones mapped the journey through life in such a way that each path would teach a truth and build a bridge to the next truth. Until you were six years old, you traveled the *Path of the Bear, named so because the bear represents the time of learning from family. On this path you learned about love and honor within the family and of your oneness with the other family members. At the age of six, you began the *Path of the Beaver. Beavers are known as animals who form a community of different families; they work together to build their homes and dams. At six you began learning from those of your community and extending your love, honor and oneness to those outside your family. Through the wisdom of your family you were allowed to go beyond your tribe and learn to love and accept the English. You are almost twelve now and near the end of the beaver path. Soon you will begin a time of preparation for the *Path of the Hawk. On this path you will learn to honor yourself. The hawk is known for its superior eyesight; the Path of the Hawk will lead you inside yourself where it is hardest to see the truth. There you will learn to see the gifts that have been given to you by the creator, and you will see how you can use these gifts for the good of all. The wisdom of the Ancient Ones will guide you on this path. The love and honor you hold for family and others will show you the way to the honor of self. Chanco, you have every right to begin now to honor yourself. The decision that you make tonight must be one that feels honorable to your spirit."

The big clock in the main hall struck four times when I went to wake Master Pace and tell him of the attack that would come at daybreak. He left Andrew and the other tenants to protect his plantation while he rowed to warn Jamestown, telling others along the way of the danger.

----

* Chanco's Indian Philosophy, The Path of the Bear, Beaver and Hawk, come from The Wheel of Life, by Howard Issac.

130

I then went to the village of my father. I stood before him and told him what I had done. I told him Master Pace had treated me as his own son, and the other members of the family had become dear to me. I could not kill Master Pace, nor could I do anything to harm the other members of the family. He squeezed my shoulder and said I should never have been asked to do such a thing.

Chapter 17

Payton awoke before daylight, having slept very little through the night. Shortly after daybreak, Opechancanough's men returned with quail and entered the Robinson's home. As Payton had hoped, they were so cocky they didn't notice the wet ground around the storage buildings or sense the expectant stillness. Moving about as usual, every eye was on the Robinson home. The animals were fed and watered, the cattle and horses were staked near the stockade.

Molly was terrified, for she knew how quickly the Indians could appear and overpower. She insisted that the women and children not wait until something happened to gather in the stockade. Reverend Swann suggested a Good Friday prayer service as an excuse to get everyone together in the stockade. Payton went to the Robinsons' and told them that the prayer bells would sound at eight for a Good Friday service in the chapel. He invited the Indians to attend, but they said they would be leaving by then. Just as the prayer bells broke the silence of the beautiful spring morning, screams could be heard from the Robinson house. The sound of the bells was then drowned out by the war whoops of the thirty or so Powhatan warriors who, seeming to appear from nowhere, rushed into the compound. Thanks to Molly, most of the women and children were already gathered into the stockade. The men fought their way in and took positions on the wall. In trying to help two of the tenants get into the stockade, Payton had received a deep slash across his shoulder and down his upper arm. The aim of the Powhatans was not only to kill but to wipe from the land anything that would aid the English in staying there. Enough men had made it to the stockade to keep the Indians from coming in, but they were helpless against the destruction taking place in the compound. The bodies of the Robinson family and three others, unrecognizable from the stockade, were brought out, piled up, and burned. Potter Ben, probably captured before he got out of

132

sight of their plantation, on the night before, was marched up from the river, where some of the warriors began to torture him, hoping to get the colonists out of the stockade. It took all of Payton's wounded strength to hold Ben's son Dan to keep him from going out to his own death. The screams coming from Payton's dearest friend were as knives cutting his own heart out. His tears fell on the back of Dan's buckskin shirt in dark splotches. Blood from the slash on Payton's upper arm mingled with the spittle and tears of the boy as he fought to break free. When Ben's cries ended with the sound of a shot, the stranglehold Payton had on the boy became an embrace and their energies mingled to support them in their unbearable pain. Another shot went off below them. There was a shriek of pain and the Indian holding the knife that dripped Ben's blood had fallen; life now convulsed from him. Ben's wife had somehow managed to break loose from those who held her and had gotten out of the stockade. She had moved far enough out to get within range and her aim had been true, with the shot for Ben and the shot for one of the warriors. "Cover her," Payton commanded as the Indians realized what had happened and rushed forward. Dan ran to her, half carrying, half dragging her through the gates of the stockade. When two more of the savages were stopped by the cover fire, the others retreated. In less than an hour Montgomery's Hundred was left in flames and ashes. Fire had been shot through the windows of Payton's house. The chapel and even parts of the stockade were on fire. The food storage buildings had stood best against the fire, but the food in them had been pillaged and strewn. Eleven were dead, Payton and two other men were wounded. Payton could not bear to think right now about those who had no warning. For he knew it was the practice of the Powhatans, using the advantage of surprise, to spread out in small parties and strike everywhere at once.

Payton lifted Molly and held her to him as she began to cry in shrill, wailing sounds. She cried for the friends of today and for the family and friends lost in a massacre that had taken place two years ago in this very same place. The shock and horror of

133

the first one had kept her suspended in numbness and unshed tears like a festering wound. Today's onslaught had reopened that wound and perhaps now it could heal. Payton thanked God that Katherine was not here today, not only for her safety but because Potter Ben had been her friend from the moment they met, and the pain he had suffered at the hands of those misguided savages would have broken her heart as it had his own. He knew those screams would forever haunt him. He thought of the child Jamie having gone through something similar watching his own mother as the victim, and he had new sympathy, praying again for his well-being. Molly, having pulled herself together, insisted on cleaning his wound. Finding soot from one of the fireplaces, scraping it down, and adding cobwebs from he knew not where, she applied them to the cleaned wound, then tightly bandaged it. Payton was thankful for the lives that had been saved by their precautions. It was nightfall before he came out of his state of shock, and melancholy settled over him. He realized he was ruined financially and so were the tenants who had worked beside him these many years. His home still smoldered, not gone, but irreparable. Some of his possessions were there, but covered in a film of black smoke with its permanent stench. Thankfully his study had been the least affected by the fire, and he was able to get his important papers out. He believed he could salvage his books. Even damaged by smoke they were valuable to him. He lay now with neither roof nor blanket to cover him, and all the losses of his life came down on him, the weight of them suffocating his pride and spirit. He wanted to give up and go home. He wanted to find Katherine, declare his love for her, and take her to a place where life could be lived without fear and sacrifice. He wanted to carry her across the threshold of his heart and learn from her how to express unconditional love, the kind he now realized to be the purest expression of the God image. He was weary of fighting for this land and of being responsible for people like the Robinsons who refused to listen to the voice of experience. Too many innocent children had died because of the ignorance of parents in the new land. He saw the smiling faces of the golden-haired Robinson children and imagined the terror of their last moment of life. Unbidden, the mangled body of his tiny daughter and the tortured body of Angela flashed through his mind's eye. He prayed for all those who had died by violent hands on this soil, red or white man. He asked that God's mercy had delivered them from the tortures of those driven by outrage. In the dark days after the death of Angela and Prissy, it had been revealed to him while in meditative state, that the spirits of the deserving leave their body before the torture and rise up to witness the violence as observers. This had given him much comfort during that time, and he called upon it again.

In the village of Chanco's family, Chanco waited in the dark by the water's edge until all was quiet and Grandmother Moon was high. "Grandmother Moon, it is I, Chanco. Thank you for helping me to make a decision last night. The massacre is over and the Pace family are safe. I do not believe that I was the cause of any of my own people getting killed. I do not know if I did the right thing or not. I only know I did what my heart told me to do. The English have lost many of their friends and families. They are filled with hatred for my people and are already making plans for revenge. Grandmother Moon, will there ever be peace between the English and the Powhatans?"

"Ah, Chanco, it has been this way with humanity since time began, and I fear it will be a long time in changing. It didn't begin with the white man and the red man coming together. You know from the experience of your mother's people that the red men did to each other all that you have seen happening between red and white. You have heard Master Pace tell of the white man's wars and violations against each other. The black men that you recently have seen being brought from ships in chains come from a land where blacks kill and enslave each other. Perhaps the very ones you have seen were sold to the slave traders by their black brothers. You have yet to learn of the yellow men and the pain they inflict upon each other. Many

135

years from now the white, red, and black man will stand together in a fight to keep the yellow men from violating each other. But will there be peace one day? Yes, Chanco, there will be peace. Some day there will be enough men like you to make it happen. Enough men who can see past the differences in color and beliefs to the oneness of all men."

Morning rose on a new day, a day for taking stock and making decisions. It was Payton's desire that everyone have a say in the process. It was decided that they would repair the long house and use it as a common shelter until they could get the food crops in the ground and the tobacco plants set. The tobacco beds, having been sown in a newly cleared area off the east field, had somehow escaped the notice of the Powhatans. The morning dew sparkled clean and fresh on the white cloth that protected each seed bed from the frost, and hope sprang anew that survival was possible.

The next few days brought news of carnage from Hampton Roads to the falls. More than a hundred miles on both sides of the James River had been ravaged by the Powhatans and the tribes Opechancanough had recruited to help. Payton mourned the loss of John Rolfe at the hands of the savages. Martin's Hundred, which Ben had been trying to reach, had suffered the heaviest losses; seventy-six had been slain. At Edward Bennett's plantation across the river, fifty-two had been slain. Berkeley Plantation, where they had met for the past two years and held Thanksgiving services, was wiped out. Even Henrico lay in ashes. Missionaries there, who had served the Indians with love and kindness, were slain. The college being built there to teach the Indians, the infirmary where they nursed the sick, and several finished and unfinished buildings, whose purpose was to benefit the Indians, were destroyed. Slaughtered there were twenty-two of the best friends the Indians had among the whites. People who Payton knew to be tireless in their efforts to gain more rights for the Indians. They came before council at every meeting with their lists of needs, begging for funds. They pleaded for equal rights for the Indians. Had their request, submitted before the January meeting of council, for the Indian's right to buy weapons, been granted, Payton knew the death tolls from this massacre would have been much higher.

There was some good news. Jamestowne had been saved, thanks to Chanco. He had been told by his brother to murder Richard Pace and steal the family's guns, but during the night Chanco came to the bedside of the man who had treated him like a son and revealed Opechancanough's plot. Pace rowed three miles across the river before dawn and alerted Jamestowne. Payton knew now why the boy had asked his advice and was thankful that Chanco had followed his heart. Mrs Proctor had successfully fought off the Indians and in spite of orders to come on in to Jamestowne in case there was more trouble, had stubbornly refused. Ralph Hamor, trader and friend to the Indians, was also attacked but was able to defend his home and save his family. The indentured Negroes who had only recently become a common sight in the colonies had been left unharmed by the Indians.

When the final count was in, the Powhatans, under the leadership of Chief Opechancanough, had destroyed the property and taken the lives of 347 colonists in an area covering both sides of the James River for a distance of 140 miles. When the Powhatans had approached Jamestowne to find the town ready and waiting, the Powhatans had retreated quickly with few or no casualties. Had they surprised and destroyed Jamestowne, it might have been the final blow for the first English colony in America.

In the aftermath of the massacre, many of the colonists followed Governor Wyatt's advice and moved into Jamestowne for protection. There, driven by revenge, a war of extermination was begun. Opechancanough had fled to the land of the Pamunkeys, leaving his people to be slaughtered by the scores and driven back into the wilderness. Payton and some of his tenants chose to stay at Montgomery's Hundred to salvage what they could of the tobacco and get some food crops in the ground. Payton's wound had become infected and was slow in healing.

He had not the energy for hate and anger, nor the desire to see anymore killing. Within a fortnight, word came from Jamestowne that the blight of war, pestilence, and famine had fallen on those gathered there. Many of the settlers, discouraged and terrified, were returning to England. The colony of almost four thousand was reduced to little more than two thousand.

Potter Ben's son, Dan, was set on returning to England. His mother had refused to go and give up their holdings. There were four children younger than Dan, and the family sorely needed him, but the death of his father had left him feeling as if life in the colony was futile. Payton knew Dan had left a sweetheart in England; Katherine had written letters for him. He thought maybe the young man needed her to help him get over this tragedy. Yet he was concerned for the family of his friend Ben with the father and the oldest son gone. Ben's wife, Nancy, was as skilled in the making of pottery as her husband had been. Maybe that would save them. Dan had made arrangements to leave on the ship that had brought Payton a letter from Katherine. It was going directly to England from here, and Payton would send an answer to Katherine by Dan. He knew he must tell her their sad news, but he was not of the heart to do that.

The massacre had left Payton weakened, not only in body but also in pride. The fear of leaving words unspoken was now greater than the fear of speaking his heart. Without restrain he wrote a letter to Katherine. He knew there was a good chance that he would never see her again, so he wanted her to know the truths that he had come to realize. In her absence he had seen that his fight against loving her had been lost from the moment he met her. "The power of my feelings for you when first I looked into your eyes was frightening. Without doubt, I knew that to love you and lose you would render to me the final blow, the blow from which there would be no recovery. What I didn't know when I was trying to keep you at arms' length was that my love for you was not an option but an absolute from that very first moment.

138

"If you haven't heard by the time Dan gets to you, he will tell you of the terrible massacre that has taken place in our colony and of the death of the Robinsons and Potter Ben. I am glad that you were not here to be exposed to the slaughter or to the shambles to which we have been reduced. We abide here as in a fog. It hurts too much to look back, and we can see nothing ahead. Reverend Swann has been our lifeline. God has given him words that speak to our higher nature. He keeps telling us that God is love, but God is law and that we must work with both if we are to make it through this. We dare not let him hear us complain, for he has told us that one of God's laws is that we must be thankful for what we have. Dwell on lack, he says, and all you will get is more lack. That serves to make one keep a tight rein on his thoughts.

"The tobacco beds were not harmed during the massacre. We have begun setting out the plants, and though we are short-handed, we have done well. We have found hard work to be the best medicine for our pain. We have been blessed with some light rains and our plants look healthy. They offer us our only chance to recover some of what we have lost.

"Though I know I may never see you again, I am truly thankful for every moment we had together. Even more thankful am I that you are there in safety. It consoles me to know that you have a place of comfort in the smallhouse and that you are being taken care of in the manner to which you are accustomed. I never want you to suffer as we have suffered here, even if it means letting you go forever. As circumstances now stand, I have nothing to offer you except your freedom from our arrangement and that is yours for the asking."

Dan was now ready and waiting for Payton to give him the letter, written on both sides of a page torn from the big ledger where he kept his accounts. Like everything else, it smelled of smoke. How Payton wished he could be the one to put this in her hand. If only he could look in her eyes and see if love still shined there for him. He longed to lie down with her and forget for a moment the weight of responsibility that lay on him. It

139

would be easier to walk away and start over with Katherine, but just as he now knew his feeling for Katherine came from a power greater than himself, he knew it was the same with the colony. This was where he was supposed to be. If he gave it up he would never find his right place again. If Katherine gave up on him, he would accept it, knowing that love such as theirs would never come again. Inside himself and in this letter he had done all he could to undo the mistakes he had made with her. It was now out of his hands. He could only pray that the same power that predestined his love for Katherine and his love for the colony, would guide him and bless him with their restoration. If not that, then the strength to accept his losses and gain from the experience.

Chapter 18

Katherine had written a letter several weeks before to notify the Montgomerys of her intended visit in mid-April. She had asked them to notify Angela's parents of her desire to visit with them also. She dared not explain anything on paper for fear that word might somehow get back to Robbie in spite of the distance. She and Jamie were excited and ready for the trip. They waited only on Carlton to say the word. For days he had put them off with one excuse after the other. On learning of their plans to sail to Tinmouth and hire a carriage to go on to Langley, Susan mentioned that her own family lived in Stanhop which was only a few miles from Langley. Carlton gained new enthusiasm for the trip on hearing of Susan's connection to that area and soon had Susan talked into going along. Katherine was sure now that she was carrying a child. Dr. Martin, coming by to check on Jamie after a mild cough, had examined her and confirmed that she was about three months pregnant. This explained the nausea that had plagued her on the ship coming home and until a week or two ago. Katherine was thrilled to know that Payton's child grew inside her. When she came back from Langley, she would give some serious thought to their future and make decisions that now had time limits. Perhaps by then her mother would be able to return home and take Katherine's place with Jamie. Jamie would give her mother exactly what she needed to continue to heal. She hated having to keep this wonderful news from her mother, when it could have helped her so. Barrister Dunbar should have everything in order soon for Jamie's claim to his inheritance.

Katherine was anxious to see how she fared on this short sailing trip in her current condition, for she knew that would affect the decisions that she was considering.

It was a wonderful spring day and everyone was in high spirits when they set out for Langley. At the docks it became obvious why Carlton had made them wait. He had found, in dry

141

dock, a ship that Katherine's father had bought before his death. Among Matthew Arlington's papers were plans to turn the former Tudor warship into a passenger and merchant ship. Repairs had already been made to the bow, where she evidently had been damaged by cannon fire. The passenger cabins had been roughed in where gun ports had formerly been on the main deck, but were not finished, The plans called for the sterncastle, topmost of the four decks, to be turned into captain's quarters. Work on that had also been roughed in when Carlton found the ship. The ship had been stripped of its forecastle due to heavy damage, and the plans called for a promenade deck to join the weather deck. Her father had designed it so that the weight of the cannons would be compensated for in the cabin materials and design. The removable blinds on the weather deck that had protected the ship's archers during battle had been turned into a decorative banister that gave passengers something to hold onto during rough weather, its extension up and around the promenade deck gave balance where the forecastle had been. Great oak timbers placed beneath the decks to support the extra weight of the guns, added to the strength of the ship and the safety of the passengers during a storm. Carlton had put as many men on the reconstruction as he felt they could afford, and from the outside she was a freshly painted beauty. Matthew's well-designed changes had taken from the ship the threatening look of a warship and had given her the look of a pleasure ship. Her name was that given to her by Katherine's father, and it stood out now with fresh paint, "Katy Two."

The beauty of the ship and the story behind it brought tears to Katherine's eyes, and she thanked Carlton again and again for his interest in carrying through with her father's plans. On board it became apparent that there was much more work to be done, but they were able to make themselves comfortable and Katherine could see that upon completion the ship would be a wonderful vehicle for long distance travel. Somehow Carlton had found Captain Brooks and talked him into coming out of retirement long enough for the short trip. He had known

Katherine when she was a child and had been a friend of her Grandfather Randolph and her father as well. The crew, all picked because they came from the Northumberland area, were being given a trip home for a few days with pay. The whole ship seemed to radiate an air of jovial goodwill and the winds were with them all the way.

At Tinmouth they had a mid-morning meal at a busy tavern, and Carlton took them to see the Roman Wall with its magnificent workmanship before setting off for the town of Langley. The road led them through rolling hills and rugged moors where sheep grazed on hillsides and wild spring flowers brightened the landscape. Katherine imagined Payton growing up here and she felt closer to him than anytime since she had left Virginia. As they grew closer to her in-laws' home Katherine began to have some misgivings about coming here. When the driver told them it was just over yon hill she took out her looking glass and straightened her bonnet, pinched her cheeks, and fluffed the curls beneath the bonnet brim. At the top of the hill they looked down on Payton's home, and she thought how he must miss being here in Spring. It was a like a painting of a pastoral scene. At the end of a long lane of blossoming pear trees stood a stately manor house of rough stone. Rising up behind it were the stone cottages and shops of a feudal village. Outbuildings and pastures completed the scene where sheep, horses, and cattle grazed in contented languor. Susan explained that the white cattle with heavy coats were Chillingham Whites, pureblood wild cattle descended from a strain that had been bred for sacrifice by the Druids. As the carriage followed the lane to the house Katherine knew that from the time they topped the hill until the carriage reached the house, the family had been aware of her coming. Jamie had been an angel the whole trip; between her and Susan they had kept him entertained during the sailing and the carriage ride. Now Katherine woke him from a nap and told him they were almost there. As soon as Carlton and Susan could politely get away, they would go on to Stanhop where Carlton would deliver Susan to her home and take a room at a nearby tavern. As they grew closer to Payton's home and family, Katherine almost wished she could go on with Carlton and Susan.

"If for any reason we are not properly welcomed here, then Jamie and I will continue on with you to the tavern in Stanhop after a short visit," Katherine said.

When the carriage pulled up in front of the house, the heavy doors flew open and by the time Katherine stepped down from the carriage with Jamie, she found herself surrounded by Payton's family. Payton's father, William, a strikingly handsome white-haired man came forth with hand out and introduced himself. He stood, grasping her hand and looking into her eyes as if he could see into her soul. Then he pulled her into a warm embrace and said, "My son has done well."

Two beautiful little girls smiled shyly at Jamie as Payton's brother came forth and cupped Katherine's hand between both of his in a warm greeting. He introduced himself as Paul, then reached a hand to his wife and brought her forth to be introduced. Lisa was beautiful, with hair of dark auburn, friendly blue eyes, and a warm smile. The two girls, Samantha and Clarissa, wanted to know who Jamie was as soon as they could gracefully acknowledge their introduction.

"This is Payton's stepson Jamie, the son of Angela; he is the reason I asked in my letter to visit with Angela's parents. I thought they should know that she left them a grandson and that a part of her still lives," Katherine said.

"Why were we not told of the child?" William asked. "It might have made things easier for Charles and Betty. I must send someone to get them now. Oh, it will gladden their hearts to know that their only child has left them a grandson, and a fine lad he is at that." Payton's father then motioned to one of the servants to come forth from where they had gathered at the door to get a look at the new Mrs. Payton Montgomery. William explained that the servants were anxious to see if there was any word as to how Payton fared and when he might come home again.

"Ask Timmy to go and fetch Charles and Betty. Tell them to come for supper."

Katherine then introduced Carlton and Susan. They declined all the offers for food and rest, asking only for the use of the toilet before they set out for Stanhop. A servant appeared at the carriage with a basket of meat, bread, cheese, and wine for them when they had finished their toilet. Katherine told the Montgomerys that Carlton and Susan would come for her and Jamie in three days, and they seemed genuinely pleased to have her.

"Father, can we not go in now and let our guests freshen up for supper? We were so excited at your arrival I'm afraid we have acted like heathen. Come on in, there is so much we are dying to know about my brother and his life in Virginia, but we will save it for the table. We have kept you too long on the doorstep," Paul said and began to shoo them all into the house where a servant waited to show Katherine and Jamie to their adjoining rooms. Because he would not have been able to get a word in edgewise, and it was not uncommon for children to be shy and quiet, no one had yet noticed that Jamie did not talk.

When Katherine and Jamie returned for supper a slender woman with hair still dark in spite of her age and a man with steel gray hair and a body kept fit through hard work had joined the family. Katherine took Jamie's hand and went right up to them. "You must be Mr. and Mrs. Mellon. I am Katherine Montgomery and this is your grandson Jamie. He has not spoken since he witnessed the massacre that took your daughter and his little sister. Jamie is being treated in London and has greatly improved in his responses. We expect that before long we will be begging him to be quiet. Jamie, this is your Grandfather and Grandmother Mellon. Remember I told you about them and how happy they would be to see you? Go give them a big hug and let them tell you about your Mama when she was a little girl."

Jamie stood looking at them with a shy smile for a moment. The two of them knelt down before him and he went to them

145

with both arms out, pulling their heads together as he squeezed them both at the same time. The Mellons were as two empty cups, filling back up with love. Katherine had sensed their restraint with each other and those around them. She knew that sorrow could cut one adrift from the very people who could give them strength. She saw Jamie bridging the gap that sorrow had wedged between them, giving to them a common joy. She saw them looking out from the darkness within to be warmed by the radiance of Jamie's trusting acceptance. She knew that something greater than her had urged her to bring them together for this reunion.

Supper was a feast and Katherine, with new appreciation, told those gathered around her of the lack in the colony of so many of the things they took for granted. They were hungry for news of Payton, so she described his plantation and told them of his position as a leader in the House of Burgesses and on the Council. She described the tobacco growing process and its importance in sustaining the colony. She explained the "head right" system of acquiring land and told stories that Payton had told her of men who came there with nothing and now owned hundreds of acres. Jamie and the two girls had been seated at a table for the children and having set for so long, they had now grown weary of being quiet and still. Even though Jamie did not speak, the attention of the girls had encouraged him to become somewhat unruly. Katherine suggested that she be given a few minutes to get Jamie ready for bed and asked if the girls could come into his room and read to him from their books or tell him a story. She explained that she would like to have a private conversation with just the family and the Mellons when she got Jamie settled. A maid was left to supervise the children and another showed Katherine to the room where the family now waited for her with curious impatience.

Settled before a fire that chased the dampness and chill from the stone house and the spring night, Katherine asked them to bear with her while she explained the string of coincidences that put Angela in the colony, pregnant with Samuel Arlington's child. She told them of her family, of her abduction and of her arrival and marriage to Payton. She stressed the danger to Jamie, if her cousin learned of his existence. She reminded them of the power of word to spread through servants and gossip. She then assured them that she trusted them to think carefully before revealing any information that could harm the boy. She told them where she was in the process of proving his inheritance and told the Mellons that she hoped that they would consider coming to London to become a part of Jamie's life when the time came. She assured them that funds would be made available to them to come back and forth if they chose or comfortable living arrangements would be made for them to live in London. Upon learning that Mr. Mellon's job as caretaker had given him such varied skills Katherine told him of the shipping firm that had been left to her and now belonged to Payton as well. She offered him a position with Carlton, explaining that he could use Mr. Mellon's experience in dealing with hired help and his wonderful carpentry and repair skills. Carlton's talents lay more in the administration of business and finance. She saw his eyes light up at the thought of new and exciting prospects in his life again. Mrs. Mellon seemed to be stunned by so much at once, but there was about her an intelligence that would process it later, and Katherine knew that Jamie had already become precious to her.

The Montgomerys were thrilled for the Mellons and assured them support in any decision they made. Katherine had, throughout the whole evening, observed her new family. Their concern and caring for Payton and the Mellons, the obvious good will between family and servants, and their gracious acceptance of her and Jamie into the family had endeared them to her. She knew they were good people and that any misunderstanding between them and Payton would give way in time to the power of love that was strong among them. Perhaps the very things that had caused them conflict had taught them to examine their true feelings, bringing to light a love for each other that was stronger and healthier. When she retired to her room at a late hour, she gave thanks for all the wonderful people who had been brought into her life since her marriage to Payton.

On the morn she was to ride with William Montgomery; she hoped to return with a better understanding of Payton's relationship with his family, and a better understanding of Payton's reluctance to express his true feelings for her.

Katherine awoke early. She got herself and Jamie ready to go down for the morning meal. William and Paul ate together from the board. Katherine fixed a plate and cup for Jamie and got him seated, then sat down beside him with her food. The weather was nice for their ride and Katherine looked forward to it. London with all of its busyness and the close quarters of their living space after the long trip back from the colony made her feel a need for the replenishment of open spaces and the beauty of nature. William and Paul had been discussing the day's business. Paul told his father to go on and enjoy the day without worrying, assuring his father that he would take care of everything. Katherine could see that William did not have full confidence in his son. She had sensed from the moment she met Paul that, likable and charming as he was, he was a man who carried responsibility lightly and would easily be distracted. It was a common thing among the gentry; the first son raised with so little discipline that he was ill prepared to take over when the time came. She wondered if Payton had always been the trustworthy son, or if living under the harsh conditions of the colony had made him so.

The Mellons came to take Jamie for the morning, and they were wonderful with him. At the stables a chestnut mare had been saddled for Katherine. Sure-footed and stout, the mare was a perfect choice for the rough terrain, Katherine thought. William was taking her to the ruins of a castle that had belonged to his ancestors. As soon as they were comfortably on the trail he began to tell Katherine of Payton's mother, who had died several years ago. "In many ways you remind me of her, she was born with all the qualities of a true lady and I suspect that you were also." They rode on in silence for a few moments

148

before he cleared his throat and began again. "Before I die I would like to look into Payton's eyes and ask his forgiveness. It would take such a load off of my heart to see that he truly forgives me. I assume he has told you that I made dreadful accusations of him and asked him to leave."

"No, sire, I am ashamed to admit that your son has told me little about his former life or his family."

"Perhaps 'tis that it hurts so much he can't, dear. After my wife had been dead for about a year I met a younger woman. I was lonely and because I wanted to believe that she loved me, she was able to fool me easily. She soon became bored with me and my lifestyle in this rather isolated area. When Payton came home she made a play for him. The more he resisted her the more she desired him. Finally when she realized that her boldness was disgusting to him, she became hostile and set out to make it look as if he had tried to seduce her. Fool that I was, I fell for it and blamed him, asking him to leave. Paul did not resist her and when I caught them together, the whole story came out. Payton is the better man of the three of us. This was not the first time I let him down as a father. Lisa was Payton's first love. When he went off to Cambridge, Paul took advantage of his absence and her youth to turn her head. I wanted the land that she would bring in marriage to my son and I feared that if Paul could turn her head another young man might also. I made the necessary arrangements in spite of my wife's disapproval and they were married. Lisa's father was more interested in marrying her to the oldest son than to the second son so it was likely that nothing would have ever come of any relationship between Payton and her, but he was hurt deeply by our betrayal. He tried not to show it but it was obvious, especially to his mother. I doubt she ever forgave me for that, and must have turned over in her grave when I banished him from his home. I have so much to answer to before I leave this world. Do you think Payton could ever forgive me?"

"I think you would find Payton a changed man from the one you knew. Life in the colony is hard; it was even harder when he first got there. He has lost his only child, his wife, and many good friends to Indians and illnesses. I love your son with all my heart and I don't believe he harbors blame. He seems to have come to an acceptance that everyone is operating to the best of their ability and that it is up to him to insulate himself from further pain or disappointment. To this end he keeps everyone at arm's length, including me. There is no more distance between us right now than there was before I left. If he finds himself weakening, he becomes more aloof. I am trying to decide whether to keep trying or give it up. I have recently learned that I am with child so my decision now affects more than the two of us and cannot be made in leisure."

"I hope you will not give up on my son. You may be his only chance for true happiness. You have, by accident or fate, been given the qualities that would appeal to Payton. He loved his mother so dearly, I believe he would measure other women by her. She had a rare quality that I can only describe as love and respect for herself and for all God's creations. She never saw herself as more than or less than any other. This is a quality that gives birth to many other desirable qualities. Not all men would recognize or appreciate those qualities. Payton could not truly love a woman without those qualities. You have them all, wrapped up in a pretty package. If any woman could get through to him, you would be she. I beg you not to overestimate this unyielding attitude he has acquired. I know Payton is not one to be close-minded. He is ever questioning and re-evaluating, even those beliefs that most of us dare not question."

"What do you mean by that, sire, beliefs we dare not question?" Katherine asked.

"Well, it was Payton's and his mother's desire that he prepare for the ministry. About two years into the ministerial courses he changed his mind. He began meeting with a group of men who questioned the traditional beliefs of our religion. I believe Sir Walter Raleigh and some of England's literary types were among those who met. I heard it called the "school of night." I don't know if that's the name they gave themselves or if it was given to

150

them by those who feared what they were doing. Payton didn't become an atheist or anything like that, he just saw so much in the teachings of the church that didn't set right with him that he began a quest of his own. He tried to explain it to me once but I wouldn't allow him to. My own beliefs were so shaky I didn't want any of the props pulled out. After my wife's death and my foolish relationship with Sara, everything I believed came tumbling down. As I began to seek a new philosophy, I came across the enlightening essays and literature of those who had dared to question and had refused to replace old dogma with new dogma. I believe that what Payton was trying to tell me back then are the things I am realizing as the truth of our being. It is so exciting when one makes a discovery that one recognizes as a truth he knew at the soul level but had forgotten at the human level. I think of Payton beginning the journey for truth at such a young age and I rejoice that he didn't wait until he was my age to begin."

"From the books in his library and his conversations with the man he chose to represent God at his plantation, he has not abandoned the search. I think you and Payton could be good friends now. Maybe you two are more alike than you ever knew. I hope the two of you get the chance to become reacquainted."

William and Katherine barely got back in time for the midday meal. The Mellons were back with Jamie. They had showed him where his mother grew up, and had let him play with the toys she had played with as a child. They had showed him a painting of Angela when she was a child, but he had been drawn immediately to the ones she had brought them not too long before she left London. Someone in Shakespeare's company had a talent for sketching and had given Angela several sketches of herself which she had brought home. Jamie had been allowed to choose one to keep, and he had run out to show Katherine as soon as she had dismounted. Jamie sat with eyelids heavy after eating only a few bites. Mrs. Mellon gathered him into her lap and pulled the tail of her apron up to cover him. She told him that if he wanted to rest his eyes a minute he could and he sank quickly into sleep.

Katherine told the family of their visit to the castle ruins, and everyone had a story to tell her of Payton's ancestors and their battles, some of which William had told her at the scene. As the morning's events and the wonderful meal settled within her, Katherine found herself feeling as Jamie must have felt, and when someone suggested they go to their room for a rest she had no objections. Mrs. Mellon carried Jamie to the room that had been given to him on the main floor and tucked him in with a kiss on his cheek. She left Katherine then, telling her they would see her at supper. Katherine removed the dusty riding habit and lay down. The next thing she knew Lisa was knocking on her door. She was shocked to learn that she had been asleep for almost two hours. Katherine was glad for this time to visit with Lisa. When the men were around they were so full of questions or stories to tell, Lisa had remained quietly in the background. She had taken a moment to put on a robe and wash her face from the water on the stand, while Lisa sat in the chair by the window looking out.

"This was Priscilla's room, when she was a young mother," Lisa told her. "She insisted on being near her sons when they were born and taking care of them. She was a wonderful person and I still miss her. You remind me of her. I wish we were going to have more time to get to know each other. It would be wonderful to have another woman here. I do get lonely sometimes for the company of women. I grew up with two sisters and I seldom see them since we all have our families now. Did William tell you about Payton and me?" she asked.

"He did mention it, but I would like to hear your side of it. He said you were both very young, and I wondered how you felt about the arrangements made for you by your father and William."

"Oh, I was such a silly child. I was flattered by the attention from Payton. He was so handsome and so sweet and good. After he was gone for awhile though, I got tired of having nothing but his letters. Paul was charming and exciting and fun. I grew up knowing that Father would choose the man I married and I accepted his choice. I was younger than Payton and I didn't realize he would be so hurt. I think now that it was pride, and the fact that Paul had always been allowed to take what he wanted from Payton. William doted on Paul, and I doubt that Paul will ever outgrow the harm it did him. Now that I am older, I look back and doubt that I truly loved either one of them. You know, in the passionate way of romance stories and such. I grew to love Payton as a dear friend and brother, and I guess I love Paul the way one would love a wayward child. I have accepted that I will never know the kind of love one reads about, but I am fortunate to have a good home, two beautiful daughters who bring me joy, and a husband who has never intentionally hurt me. I suspect that when one is married to a man such as Paul, it helps if one doesn't feel an obsessive love. He is ever chasing new gratifications. They are so different, Payton and Paul. Payton ever looks inward for his gratification, and Paul ever looks to things outside himself. Tell me, do you love Payton in the way of storybook romances? It is so like a storybook romance, the way you two came together and were married the very next day."

"I was prepared to dislike any man who came for me under such circumstances, but something happened the moment Payton appeared. It was as if he was someone I already knew and loved. I can't explain it; it is something beyond the reasoning of the mind. My heart recognized him and rushed to embrace him while I stood back in amazement. What happened to me the moment I looked into Payton Montgomery's eyes was so absurd that a writer of romance would be afraid his readers would not find it plausible. I don't find it plausible myself, but I accept Payton as my heart's desire. When I left him in the colony, I feared that he had detached himself from love forever. The Payton you knew has had so much heartache, added to that which he carried with him from here. It's as if his heart has become encased in armor as a shield against the pain of loss.

153

Although I left because of the pressing business with Jamie, the strain of loving someone who does not return your love is not what I would choose for a lifetime. A letter that I received from Payton has given me reason to believe that his armor did not serve him as well as he thought. Perhaps it took my absence to make him aware that love is worth the risk involved."

"For Payton and yourself I hope it is so. Also I want to believe that storybook romances do happen in this world. It is hard for me to imagine Payton becoming cold and hard. He is the beloved among everyone here, because he cared so for others."

"I have just learned that Payton and myself are no longer the only ones involved. A child grows within me who needs the love of father and mother."

Lisa was excited over this news and eager to answer any questions that Katherine might have concerning her pregnancy. One question led to another and Jamie awoke and was taken to the nursery by the girls while they continued talking until the supper bell rang. As Katherine hurried to dress for supper she regretted that she would not have more time with Lisa. She had few really good friends in her life and she felt that Lisa could have been a very special one. Before she left she would tell Lisa how much she wanted them to remain friends and suggest that they write to each other as often as possible.

At supper Lisa seemed to have become somewhat withdrawn, and Paul seemed a little less friendly toward Katherine. When William suggested a toast to the babe who, if male, might someday be heir to the Montgomery Manor, Katherine felt as though she had been hit in the stomach. It wasn't fair that inheritance should have the power to create such rivalry among families. Her own family was gone because of it, and now it had reared its ugly head in this house. "If it is indeed a son that I carry, his inheritance will be secured in the colony of Virginia. Lisa has produced two healthy girls with no serious problems and now has the incentive to try again. Let's offer a toast to cousins and heirs on both sides of the ocean."

The Mellons had been invited for supper and to spend time with Jamie. He was now comfortable and loving with them and they with him. Katherine wished they were going to have more time together and hoped they would come to London. She treasured the time she had with her grandfather and felt she had gained much from his love and acceptance of her.

There was much to be done around the manor at this time of the year, so Lisa and Katherine were able to spend most of the next day together. She was still a bit reserved but Katherine knew it was Paul's worry and not Lisa's that had caused the tension. Lisa seemed to carry the attitude that it didn't matter who owned anything as long as everyone shared in the enjoyment of it.

That evening it was time to get packed and prepare to leave. Carlton and Susan would pick them up early the next morning. When the Mellons came to say good-bye, they told Katherine they had decided to come to London, but that their help would be needed here until late summer. William had told them they would always have a place at the manor in case they didn't like the city. If Katherine would make preparations for them they would come at the end of August. Charles would begin working with Carlton, and Betty would be available to take care of Jamie anytime that she was needed. If Katherine could find them a small cottage, they thought they might enjoy living in London. Both of them held the excitement of children in their eyes, and Katherine could see that this was a great adventure for them.

They each took one of Katherine's hands to thank her. "A few days ago our life was bleak and empty. You have given us so much, we don't know how to thank you," Charles told her and Betty nodded in agreement.

"I am only giving back to you what was already yours. Jamie was given to you by your daughter, but circumstances took him away. Were it not for the interference of my cousin Robbie, things would have followed a different course and you might have been living in London right now with daughter and grandson. I am so sorry for what we have all lost to his greed. I

155

can only trust that everyone concerned has grown from this in the ways that God would have us grow. I beg you again, please be careful in what you say and do as you prepare to leave here. We could not stand to lose Jamie too."

After supper William asked to talk to Katherine in private. When she went into his study he gave her a letter to deliver to Payton. He then told her that she was welcome to leave Jamie there until his inheritance was settled. When she declined he asked if there was any way he might help to speed it up. She assured him that everything that could be done was being done. Her barrister had the marriage certificate, the birth certificate and Payton's verification that he had been named guardian by Angela. William gave her a note that he had written to an Inspector Keller. He knew this inspector and knew that she could trust him to investigate the death of her brother and father.

Katherine had told William that she would go and see Inspector Keller as soon as she got back to London. Through God and new understanding of God's laws she had let go of the hate and anger that she felt toward Robbie. The light of this new awareness had made her more compassionate toward him, making her realize that it was only the grace of the One Power that kept us all from living in such darkness. She would do all that she felt led to do in order to protect Jamie and herself and leave Robbie to a higher justice.

Carlton and Susan were there just after daybreak, and Katherine could see that they had grown even closer during their time with Susan's family. At Tinmouth they refreshed themselves at an inn and returned the carriage before hiring a smallboat to take them out to the Katy Two. Katherine marveled at her beauty from the shore and was amazed that her father's small changes had given such a different look to what had once been a threat to the enemies of England. The Katy Two was not as large as some of the Tudor war ships. It had been her job to give chase when the enemy turned tail. She must have been a powerful little lady in her day. How wonderful that she could offer comfort and pleasure in her old age.

Chapter 19

Betty Mellon had a cousin in London. When they were children, they had been close. Through the years they had kept in contact through letters once or twice a year. It gave her comfort to know there was someone in London that she knew. She looked forward to becoming reacquainted with Margaret. Margaret, like her, had only one child, a boy named Ewell. From what she had gathered from the few times she had seen them, and from reading between the lines of Margaret's letters, Ewell was a handful. Margaret had loved him too much. She had let him take over his own management, bending to his will on every issue. Betty's own mother had told her when Angela had been born that God puts a child in our hands for training and safe-keeping. It is on loan to us, not to fulfill any selfish needs that we might have, but to be guided to self-reliance and the development of potential. Betty herself had fallen prey to Angela's wiles through the years and Charles more often than her, but neither of them had let Angela become the master of the house as Ewell appeared to be. Betty was now curious to see how he had turned out. As she sat down to get a letter ready for posting to Margaret she debated on how much she could safely explain to her cousin about their decision to move to London. She wanted so to tell Margaret about her darling grandson and how those heathen Indians had struck her yet another blow by rendering her grandson mute. How could it possibly put Jamie in danger to tell Margaret about her grandson if she mentioned not the name of Jamie's father or the child's association with anyone in London? Margaret had known of Angela's marriage to Payton, she would naturally assume Jamie to be Payton's son. Betty decided she wouldn't mention Jamie's age so as to foster that notion until Margaret could be told otherwise. After the letter had been posted, Betty had some misgivings, at least enough so as not to mention the letter to Charles.

157

When the letter arrived in London Margaret had gone to the market. Ewell removed the seal and read the letter. He threw it back on the mail tray, got dressed and left the house. He knew a gentleman in Whitehall who might be interested in this bit of information. He had collected small coin over the years by providing the gentleman with information concerning his cousin Angela. He had set out to see what the cad was up to and milk that for some real quid. When the gentleman became master of a large estate a few months ago, the pieces fell together, and he had been ready to pluck the goose. Then a fellow that he knew, named Charley, was fished out of the Thames. The very same fellow the gentleman had hired to arrange an accident for him several years back. If the recent death of Charley had been connected to the gentleman in question, and Ewell had reason to believe it did, then the fellow must have tried something similar to what Ewell had in mind. This had given Ewell cause to reconsider the risk in trying to blackmail such a ruthless gentleman. For now he would use this new information to gain a stake at the gaming tables tonight. He would tantalize Master Arlington by making the information seem more important to the gentleman than it really was. By having put together the whole plot, Ewell knew that the mention of a son would alarm the gentleman. Ewell would act as if he didn't know whether it was important or not, then insist on a crown when the gentleman reacted as he knew he would. By the time he discovered the boy to be too young, Ewell would have had his chance at the tables again, maybe with enough luck to have turned the crown into real quid.

Ewell was seated in the library across from Master Robert Arlington. The gentleman looked at him as if he were a fly, come back to plague him. "My mother received a letter this morning from Angela's mother saying that they would be moving to London soon to be near her grandson that had just come home from America. I wondered if this might be of interest to ye?"

"How could that possibly interest me?" he asked.

158

"Well, sire, ye said I was to come to ye with any news about Angela, that ye would be the judge of whether it was of any use to ye or not. I'm just here to do yer bidding."

"In truth, this news is about Angela's mother. I thought I made it clear that Angela's death put an end to any business I had with you."

"Yes, sire ye did at that. But ye see, Angela was an only child and any grandson would have to come from her." Ewell gloated to himself as he saw realization slowly begin to dawn on the cad. "I can see that this is of no consequence to ye, and that I shouldn't have disturbed ye. Please accept my apology, sire," Ewell said and stood to leave.

The gentleman made a motion for Ewell to sit back down. "Tell me", he began.

Now was Ewell's chance to show this bastard how it feels to be the lick-spittle. "Sire, I will no longer subject myself to insult. 'Twas a different face ye put on when first ye came to seek my favor, and naught was said when you reduced me to an underpaid hireling. They's times it cost me more to bring ye word of Angela than the few coins ye dropped in me hand. Today I have become no better than a beggar at ye door. And a fine door it is that ye now sit behind. 'Tis but a fool I've been on a fool's errand. I will bid you good day, sire, and take my leave." Ewell now standing, turned and walked toward the door.

"I beg your forgiveness, perhaps a crown would restore our friendship," he said with some sarcasm. "One crown today and two more when a description of the boy has been rendered. As a cousin to the child, you should be able to find him and get a look at him. I want to know the boy's age, how he came to be in London, and who is responsible for him now." He took from his pocket a crown, handed it to Ewell, and showed him to the door.

Ewell's little speech had stirred within himself a real anger. Once put out before him, he could see the truth of his words. He would learn what there was to learn about this matter and if there was indeed something for the gentleman to fear, he might just knock Mr. Arlington off that high horse and endear himself to some well-off kin at the same time. He squeezed the crown in his pocket and stepped up his pace with a tune.

It took him three days to discover where the child was being kept. The new Mrs. Montgomery, who by some twist of fate was the sister of Samuel Arlington, had brought the child from the colonies. No one that he could find had set eyes on the child, so Ewell still did not know if it was possible the child was the rightful heir to Robert Arlington's ill-gained fortune. When this rainy weather let up he would watch the enclosed garden to see if the child was brought out to play. In the meantime he would find out what he could about the Lady Montgomery. In order to live by one's wits, one often had to do some vile things, but to set his own cousin up to be murdered, and him a child at that, was stooping low, even for a knave like himself. Besides, the gentleman had pushed his luck already. Sooner or later he was going to slip up and Ewell knew how it was when gentlemen got caught. Anyone with even the slightest connection could be fingered as the scapegoat. Anyone who knew enough to point the finger in the right direction could end up in the Thames, like poor Charley. Ewell would see the child, eliminate him as a threat to the gentleman, and collect the two crowns. If by chance the boy was a threat, Ewell would figure out how to handle that to his greatest advantage.

Chapter 20

Following their return to London, Katherine had begun to
consider the future. Until Jamie was safely settled she didn't see
how she could take action on the plans that were formulating in
her mind, but she could make preparations. She now knew that
her place was with Payton, and she had a burning desire to see
their child born on Virginia soil. Payton was much on her mind.
She had read the letter from him over and over, and she sensed
the feeling that had gone into his words. She could tell that he
was afraid that Carlton might mean more to her than a friend and
that he feared they might not realize the danger for Jamie and
herself. She knew, with a knowing that went deeper than her
mind, that every word of his explanation about Samuel and her
father was true. After he had explained that, as best one could in
a letter, it seemed he had tried to let her know how much he
cared and wanted her, while allowing her to make the decision
that was best for her. She had given much thought to her life in
the colony. There had been more purpose and fulfillment there
than she had ever known. She had awakened every morning
with the excitement of knowing that what she was doing was
important and mattered to the floundering colony. Just the fact
that she believed, with Payton, in what they were doing, had
given strength to the dreams of those around them. In America,
she had seen those ready to accept more for themselves than
their mother country would ever allow them. Some wanted land
of their own and those things they associated with landed
gentlemen. It was the duty of those who had already been
blessed with the things they sought, to make them aware of the
responsibility that comes with ownership. Others wanted the
freedom to choose a religion that was right for them. Perhaps
men like Reverend Swann could help them learn to separate the
wheat from the chaff. He had certainly made her begin to see
God in a new light.

In spite of his efforts to appear invincible, Payton needed her more than he knew. The time she had spent away from him had made her certain that she never wanted to be separated from him again. Yes, she belonged in America and as soon as the affairs concerning Jamie were settled she would return to her husband. When next she saw Carlton she would ask him to put enough men on the Katy Two to have it ready for her trip home.

Katherine had written to her mother the day after she had talked to Robbie. She had assured her mother that she, Roberta, and Arthur were fine. She had told her that they were comfortable in Aunt Katherine's smallhouse and that Cooke Della came every day but Sunday to cook for them. She wasn't sure how much she could tell her without upsetting her, so she made her note short, not even telling her of her marriage to Payton. She had wished so that she could tell her mother about Jamie, but she wasn't sure of her mother's condition and knew not if her mail would go directly to her or through some of the staff to be inspected.

Once her intention of returning to Payton was clear in her mind, it was if everything began to happen at once to help bring it about. First, Katherine's Aunt Rachel, Robbie's mother, sent a boy around to see if Katherine could receive her for a short visit. After Arthur and Jamie were sent out for a ride in Samuel's buggy, Roberta received Aunt Rachael and led her to the parlor. When Katherine entered, Aunt Rachael stood with genuine feeling and gave her a hug. Katherine felt a pang of guilt over what she was about to do to this woman's only son. Roberta brought them refreshments and then Aunt Rachael got down to the purpose of her visit. Rachael had received notice from Doctor Sanford that Katherine's mother, Marie, was responding well to the experimental program of the sanatorium, and that he would like to place her back in her home soon with careful monitoring. He had predicted that two to three weeks should have her prepared for her return home. Aunt Rachael also had news of Thomas Barlow that came as a relief. When Robbie had first asked Mr. Barlow to leave, he had put up a fuss and made several threats. He had also insisted on his right to visit his "dear wife." At first he had come every few days for a supervised visit; then he had begun to slack off. One day Aunt Rachael was called upon by an elderly gentleman from Cornwall who carried with him a likeness of Thomas Barlow. This gentleman claimed that Thomas Barlow had married his daughter shortly after she was widowed and had almost brought about her death by giving her large doses of laudanum, and her with a heart ailment. When the gentleman had come to the aid of his daughter and begun to have Mr. Barlow investigated, Mr. Barlow had disappeared. Evidently Mr. Barlow had learned of the gentleman having been around Whitehall asking questions, for Rachael had not seen or heard from him since before Marie was taken away. This man's investigation had turned up several other widows that had also been used by Thomas Barlow; thus, his marriage to Marie was never a legal marriage, for which Katherine and Rachael were relieved.

Two days later Katherine received a message from Arnold Dunbar that everything was in order for Jamie to claim his inheritance. The papers had been filed with the proper authorities and had been approved. Robbie would receive notice within ten days and be given thirty days to vacate the premises.

May had brought with it some sunshine and warm weather. Jamie had been outside enough to get some color in his cheeks and though he still was not talking, he often giggled and squealed when Arthur or one of the others played games with him. It was into the second week of May when the stranger came with the news that terrified them. He introduced himself as a cousin of Betty Mellon and asked to talk to Lady Montgomery alone. Katherine took him into the parlor.

"My name is Ewell, mum, and a few weeks ago I was hired by a gentleman to watch this house and find out all I could about the little boy that lives here and sometimes plays in your garden. Because I was Angela's first cousin, the gentleman has hired me in the past to find out things for 'em, but I didn't know then wot I know now. Me own mother got a letter from Betty that says they

163

will be moving to London to be with their grandson. This lad is me own kin, and even if 'e wer'nt I can't be a party to murder. This man is a mean and dangerous man. 'Tis putting me life on the line I am to tell ye this. The same gentleman hired an acquaintance of mine a few years back to arrange an accident for 'em. Me acquaintance was later found floating in the Thames. Do ye know this man and why 'e might have something against me cousin's child, mum?"

"Is the man's name Robert Arlington?" Katherine asked.

"Yes, mum, 'tis the very same," Ewell answered.

"The man is my cousin and it appears that he has killed my brother and my father in order to inherit the Arlington estate. Now my nephew, which was born of my brother and Angela, is the rightful heir and his life is in grave danger. I appreciate you coming to me. What can I do to stop this madness?"

"I have yet to report to 'em on the boy. I could tell 'em the boy is but a babe. Thing is, 'e may not take me word for it and do a double check. The only way I can see that ye would know fer sure the boy was safe is to set a trap and catch the knave."

"Yes, that is what I would like to do. My cousin deserves to pay for what he has done to my family. If you are willing to help me I will make it worth your while. I would like you to go back to Robbie and tell him that the boy looks to be about five years old. Tell him you were able to see through a window that the boy sleeps in the bottom bedroom on the east side of the house. The sooner we can get him to act, the better, for I will have to place Jamie somewhere and keep the whole place guarded."

"Aye, mum, I will tell 'em that the boy is a spitting image of the man wot courted me cousin Angela, and I will add that I talked to a servant and 'tis likely ye will be taking the boy back to the colony in a few days. That should put a fire under 'em to get the job done. 'Twill be after six this evening afore I can talk to the gentleman. That will give ye time to set the trap."

After Ewell left, Katherine sent a message around to Carlton asking him to hire two or three reliable men to guard her home and to bring them as soon as possible. She sent a message to

Susan telling her that what they had feared concerning Jamie had come about and that she needed her help. She then called Arthur, Roberta, and Cooke together and explained what had happened. She told them that there was no telling what action her cousin might take, that he could set fire to the house or decide to kill everyone in it. She would ask Susan to take Jamie to her home and keep him there until this was over. She asked Arthur to go with Jamie to watch over him in case something should go wrong. A guard would be posted outside at Susan's to keep the watch. Roberta insisted on staying with Katherine, and Cooke would follow her usual routine of staying during the day and going home to her husband at night.

Carlton arrived in time for the midday meal. Once told of Ewell's visit and the plans that Katherine had made so far, he began to raise questions that had not occurred to Katherine.

"What if this Ewell is still working with Robbie, and this is some trick to get Jamie away from us? What if Robbie hires someone to come and manages to keep himself from being implicated when we catch the one who comes? Katherine, you have set into motion a dangerous plan. You must let me contact the proper authorities. We need the help of men experienced in this type of intrigue. The word of men in authority would be more credible in the event that Robbie is caught in the act. The bobby assigned to night watch down at the shipyard is a fine chap. His father is Inspector Keller, the one assigned to investigate your father's death. The boy told me just recently that his father had never been satisfied to rule Matthew's death an accident, but he had been unable to come up with enough to prove otherwise."

"I'm sorry, Carlton, you're right of course. I am just so tired of worrying about Jamie and this whole mess, I have acted without thinking. Please get Inspector Keller as soon as you can. This is the same man that Payton's father told me I could trust. I also have that note to give him from William. Tell the inspector that Ewell told me Robbie had hired an acquaintance of his named Charley to arrange an accident a few years ago. Charley

165

was later found dead in the Thames. Ewell was telling me this to make me understand how dangerous Robbie could be. Tell him how Samuel was killed first, and how the man who was supposed to have killed my brother in a duel was out to sea when that took place. Explain to him that Payton wrote my father from the colony and suggested that Robbie may have been to blame for Samuel's death. It was after my father became suspicious of Robbie that he was killed. If the inspector understands the whole story, he will see the urgency of our situation. Ewell said it would be after six this evening before he would see Robbie, but I will be terrified until we do something to protect Jamie. We will let Inspector Keller advise us on where to place Jamie and let them keep him under guard."

Chapter 21

After Ewell left with his two crowns, Robbie sat considering this new threat to his fortune. He could hardly believe that Samuel and Angela had conceived a child and that he had not learned of it until now. He thought of Katherine's visit to him and wondered just how much she knew and how much she suspected. Since she had married the same man whom Angela had been married to, he would have to assume she knew too much. He had decided he would take care of the child and Katherine himself. When Charley had shown up at his door trying to blackmail him, he had realized the danger of involving anyone else in business such as this. Charley had threatened him, saying it was all written down. That had worried Robbie for months after Charley's death, for he knew not with whom or where Charley may have left a written record. He did know that Charley had never learned to write and had finally decided that Charley had been bluffing. When the time was right, he would have to get rid of Ewell, just as he had gotten rid of Charley.

Ewell was too smart for his own good. Robbie had known as soon as the bastard reminded him that Angela was an only child; Ewell had pretty much figured things out. Once he got rid of Katherine and the child, Ewell would be a double threat. Well tomorrow night he would take care of the child and cousin Katherine, for they were the most immediate threat. He might finish in time to catch Ewell on his way home from the gaming tables. It was not uncommon for an intoxicated man to get mugged after leaving the tables. That would put an end to it. Robbie was ready to put himself forward as the new master. He had never wanted to kill Uncle Matthew. That's why he had hired it done. His uncle had always been kind, even after he became suspicious and started asking questions. 'Twas Samuel's place he had wanted to take, with Uncle Matthew and the rest. Robbie had spent his whole life in Samuel's shadow, just because he had been born to the wrong brother. Samuel had been

167

everyone's prince. If their situations had been reversed, Robbie would have been the one on whom they all doted.

Samuel's child would be easy. Ewell had told him where the child slept. He couldn't leave Samuel's son to chance. He would smother the child before he set the place on fire; then if the boy happened to be pulled out they would think the smoke did it. He wanted also to finish something he had started a long time ago with Katherine. Thought she was too good for him to touch her. He felt his organ rise at the thought of it. His fantasy would finally come true. For a while there, when Mr. Barlow was trying to trade her off to every man in town, it looked doubtful. He had thought that with Matthew gone he would move right in as master of the house and she would bend to his will. He hadn't counted on it taking so long, and Marie getting married in between. The fire would start in her room, after he was through with her. It was good that things had worked out this way. Served her right, always took up for Samuel, she did, even when Samuel was wrong. After Robbie had satisfied himself with Katherine, the problem he had with other women would be gone; he was sure of it. Too bad that Montgomery fellow got to her first. Ewell had said there was only her and two old servants. Robbie knew that the servants' quarters were upstairs, and that Katherine would have taken Aunt Katherine's room next to the one where the boy slept. The big decorative key to Aunt Katherine's smallhouse had hung downstairs with the others at the Whitehall estate for as far back as he could remember. After tomorrow night he would again be the only heir to the Arlington estates and from then on he would be regarded, by all of London, as Samuel had been. As an added benefit, he would have fulfilled the fantasy that had served to give him the only sexual experience he had ever known. He put his hand on his organ and release came within seconds. After tomorrow night he would be able to make his fantasies real with any woman he chose.

Inspector Keller's men had changed to the shift that had been in place on the night before at the smallhouse where the child lived. Under guard also was the home of the boy's nurse, where they were hiding Jamie. The inspector had known Matthew Arlington well. In fact the gentleman had come to him after the death of his son Samuel and suggested that the shot that killed his son, had been fired from too close to have been a duel. He had known that Matthew was onto something, but when he refused to implicate anyone or give him anything to work with, Inspector Keller had no choice but to wait until he was ready to confide in him. At least he now had the opportunity to prove that his intuitive feeling concerning Matthew's death had been correct. He was a man who had learned to rely heavily on his intuitive powers, and those powers had told him at the time that Matthew's death was not accidental. Often it was not only his own life, but the lives of the men who served under him, including his own son, that depended on his intuitive feelings. He could not afford to lose faith in those powers. He hoped that this night's work would clear three murder cases from his books and prevent another. Of course, Samuel Arlington's death had never been classified as a murder and Matthew's had been ruled an accident, except in the mind of the inspector. Charley Duncan, however, was a clear case of murder and though the world was better for it, a crime had been committed and it was his duty to see it through.

He had heard the clock on the tower strike eleven a few moments ago. He didn't expect the Arlington boy to make his move before midnight. As it turned out it was no more than five minutes after midnight when a heavy figure made its way confidently toward the smallhouse. As he drew close to the house being watched, he walked brazenly to the door, put a key in the lock, then went in as though he owned the place. Inspector Keller knew his own son and the others were capable of handling the situation from the inside. He had given orders that they were to let Robbie get all the way to the bed where the child-sized dummy lay. What they wanted was a clear case of attempted murder. Inside, Tommie Keller watched the intruder make his way to the child's room and with gloved hands take a cushion from the rocker beside the bed. As he moved to press it on the face of the mannequin, Tommie pushed a gun into his back and told Robbie to put the cushion down and turn around. Instead, Robbie turned, whacked the gun aside with the cushion, and ran. He ignored the calls of the two men at the door for him to stop. Tommie, thinking to fire a warning shot, aimed at the floor and shot. At that very same instant, the man guarding the front door tackled Robbie and pushed him into the lead from the gun. Robbie convulsed three or four times as he lay on the floor and then went before a higher court than man's. By the time Katherine and the others returned from Susan's the men had cleaned up the blood, and there was no sign of what had taken place. Robert Simpson Arlington had been shot resisting arrest after attempting to murder a five-year-old boy. A London newspaper that had recently begun circulating at weekly intervals, carried the whole story. It told that Robbie was suspected of killing the grandfather and the father of the child that he had intended to smother to death. The day after the story came out, Charley Duncan's sister presented Inspector Keller with Charley's statement that he had been responsible for the accident that took Matthew Arlington's life, having been paid to do this by Robert Arlington. The girl had been afraid to come forth with the information before Robbie's death, especially since it could help her brother in no way. As to Samuel's death they could only surmise that Robbie had shot Samuel when Payton didn't show for the duel. At last it was over and Katherine could soon go to Payton.

Chapter 22

Katherine, Jamie, and the servants had moved into the house at Whitehall. The smallhouse was being made ready for Charles and Betty Mellon, even though they would not move in until late August. Carlton had hired a crew of workmen to put on the Katy Two, and progress was beginning to show. Marie Arlington was returning home today from Dr. Sanford's sanatorium and judging from the last note Katherine had received from her mother, she was much like her old self, the self before Samuel's death. Katherine still had not told Marie about Jamie; nothing had been resolved when last Katherine wrote to her. Then everything had happened so fast and it was so close to time for her mother's release, there was not time for a letter to reach her. She had told Marie, in her last note to her, that a surprise, more wonderful than anything she could imagine, awaited her at home. Dr. Sanford had written to say that Marie was being released and that he would accompany her on the coach, as he had business in London and Marie wanted him with her when she faced her family. When a hired carriage was let through the gates by Arthur that afternoon, Katherine saw it stop and Marie got out and embraced Arthur; she then got back in and rode to the front door. Katherine, Carlton, Susan, and Roberta were there to meet her. Katherine wanted to prepare Marie for Jamie before she introduced him; Cooke Della had him occupied in the kitchen. Katherine saw immediately that Marie had gained weight and looked ten years younger than when she had last seen her. Dr. Sanford hovered near her as she embraced Katherine and Roberta. Upon seeing Carlton, she was as happy to see him as if he had been a son, so close had he been to their family. Katherine then introduced Susan as Carlton's future bride and as nurse to Marie's grandson. Marie looked puzzled and Katherine asked her to be seated in a nearby chair. Katherine then related the story of her kidnaping, her marriage to Payton, and her discovery of Payton's stepson. She told her mother that Jamie

171

could not talk and explained why, how she had loved him from the moment she saw him and had felt a special kinship to him. Marie broke in at this point.

"Katherine dear, you know that your husband's stepson is just as welcome here as any child will ever be, and that he will be accepted by me as a grandson if that is what you want."

"No, Mother, you must let me finish my story. It gets even better." Katherine then told her about Carlton showing up at their plantation and recognizing Jamie immediately as Samuel's son.

"Oh, Katherine, how could that be? It is not possible," her mother interrupted.

"Cooke Della, bring Jamie here and let Mother see for herself."

Jamie hung back shyly as Cooke Della urged him forward; Marie Arlington looked as if she might faint. "I don't know how it can be, but this child is as much like Samuel when he was that age as two peas in a pod. "Come to me child, sit here by me while Katherine explains this to me."

"Mother, here is Jamie's birth certificate. See, Samuel James Arlington. Here is a certificate of marriage, signed by your son Samuel two days before he died. Here is a paper drawn up to appoint my husband, Payton Montgomery as legal guardian."

Marie Arlington was now crying. "Katherine, this is truly the most wonderful gift that I could ever ask for. I only wish your father had known."

Dr. Sanford took Marie's hand and spoke softly to her, "Marie, dear, I must leave now in order to make my appointment. I know that you are going to be just fine, you have everything you need for healing. If I am not mistaken, I believe there may be even more grandchildren in your future." He then looked at Katherine and winked.

"How did you know," Katherine gasped. She then looked at her startled mother.

"My goodness, I don't know if I can stand any more surprises. Is it true, Katherine, are you with child?"

Katherine then confessed that it was true, and Marie wanted to hear all about her husband, and about the girl that Samuel had secretly married, and about the connection between Payton and Angela.   Because this would lead to the horrid truth about Robbie, and Katherine wasn't sure her mother was ready for that she suggested that they leave that until later and get her settled, but Marie refused to wait.

Katherine told Marie just enough to pacify her.   There was no way to avoid telling her that Robbie was dead.   She then wanted to know where Rachael was.   She wanted to thank her for her help.   She felt that Rachael had perhaps saved her life, and now she needed them.   Katherine, not sure what Aunt Rachael would feel toward them now, told Marie that Rachael had gone to visit her sister.   Katherine ached as she remembered Aunt Rachael falling apart at the funeral, her sister and brother-in-law supporting Rachael as they left.

Finally, Marie, exhausted from the trip and so many surprises, was persuaded to give Jamie and Katherine one last hug and go to her room to rest.   Katherine gave her mother a few days to adjust to the positive changes in her life before she broke the news that Robbie had been responsible for Samuel's death and her father's.   Just as Katherine had suspected, her mother quickly grasped the implications and the story of his intentions to murder Jamie had to be told.   Marie mourned, as Katherine had, the death of Robbie and the effect of his crimes on the Arlington family.   They grieved also for Rachael and the terrible shock of all this at once.   Katherine thought Aunt Rachael might harbor some hurt or anger toward her, since she was connected with the set-up that ended Robbie's life.   They decided that Marie should be the one to write Aunt Rachael, thanking her for all she had done for Marie and assuring her that she would be welcome at her home anytime.

On the eighteenth day of June, Katherine was called from the garden to receive a caller who waited for her in the library. Roberta's turned up nose suggested the caller to be someone of whom she did not approve. In the library Katherine found Potter

173

Ben's son, Dan, standing uncomfortable with cap in hand. A handsome lad, merry and full of life when she left, he now stood before her a shadow of his former self. Her heart plummeted in dread of what was to come. Katherine went straight to him and hugged him to her. He broke down in her embrace; the minutes it took him to regain his composure were the longest and the most fearful of any Katherine had ever experienced.

"The Indians," he said, sucking the mucous and the heartache back to start again.

Katherine, now wanting to delay what he was going to tell her, took her handkerchief from her pocket and held it to his nose. "Blow," she said, then, "It's Payton, isn't it. Is Payton dead?"

With head bowed into the handkerchief, he shook it from side to side and Katherine knew she could take anything he had to tell her if Payton was alive.

After the story was told, they cried in each other's arms. Then Dan made as if to go.

"Where do you plan to go from here?" Katherine asked him.

"My only thought right now is to go to Melinda. I will marry her and go to work for her father, if they will have me."

"How about your family and the dreams your father had for them and you?"

"I never want to see that place again. It's never going to get any better, the killing, the burning. I don't want to spend my life in that."

"Dan, I have a ship being prepared to take me back. After you go and talk to Melinda, after you have had some time to think, I beg you to return with me. Take Melinda and any of her family that will go with us. If you decide not to go with me, at least come back and help me gather supplies and men to take with me. I need someone to go to the debtors' prison and buy out some of the decent families. I need someone to help me purchase the necessary tools and supplies for starting over. I have no one who can help me with that. I will hire you and pay you well. It will be about two weeks before I can leave. Take a week to rest and think, then come back for there is much to do."

Katherine kissed his cheek and bade him have a bite to eat and speak to Jamie before he left.

Just as Dan was ready to leave he remembered the sealed envelope that Payton had sent to Katherine. He took it from the baggage he had left by the door, and Katherine went to her room to open it as soon as they said their good-byes. The letter from Payton confirmed that her decisions about him had been right. Everything she had hoped to hear from him was there, but it gave her little joy. The letter was from a Payton that had been stripped of all pride and confidence. Between the lines of his letter she could feel his discouragement. His desolation was so tangible, it choked her. Her heart ached for him and all that he had been through. It amazed her that this man had never once, even now when he was financially ruined, mentioned the money or possessions that might be due him through his marriage to her. Now that things were settled concerning Jamie and he had her mother, his other grandparents coming, and Susan who would see to his care, Katherine longed to be on her way to Payton. He needed her right now and she could not get to him. It would still be months before she could comfort him and hearten him with the news of their baby. Fear gripped Katherine as she thought about Payton's wound and the dear ones God had taken from her. No, she thought, I will not allow myself to compare the past with the future. I know God will keep Payton safe until I can get there and in spite of the arguments of all my loved ones, I know God will help me and my baby make it to Virginia soil. Katherine then made herself a promise that she would never leave Payton again. Until now, she had kept him pushed to the back of her mind while she tended to the duties and obligations she owed to her family. Only at night when she went to bed did she allow herself to feel the desire and yearn for his touch, to imagine his body next to hers. She would picture his face, his smile, his eyes. This letter had brought the full impact of her

175

oneness with him. She sensed that circumstances were so bad in the colony and that his despair was so great, he believed, like Dan, that things were beyond remedy. Thinking thus, he loved her enough that he was willing to give her up, rather than have her go down with him. She would not be able to push him to the back of her mind any longer; the urgency to get back to him would stay with her day and night.

Katherine, knowing that the Mellons would not come to London before August or September, put Dan and his new wife up in the smallhouse for the week that he would be working for her in London. She believed Dan needed time to be alone with his new wife. Dan had found Melinda's father on the verge of being sent to debtors' prison himself. The king, unable to raise taxes without the consent of Parliament and unwilling to work with them, had raised tariffs and made laws that were driving anyone connected to the wool and clothing business into bankruptcy. Melinda's father was among them. After a week with them Dan had returned saying that Melinda and eight of her family were so excited about going to the colony that nothing he could say would change their mind. He acted as if he had grudgingly been forced to reconsider, but Katherine knew that he would never be happy with his mother and younger brothers and sisters struggling without him in Virginia.

The day after Dan had brought her the news of the Jamestowne massacre, Katherine had written to the Mellons and told them of the smallhouse and that it would be ready for them anytime after the first week of July. She also told them, she would not be there to greet them as she would be leaving within two weeks to return to the colony. She explained about the massacre and that supplies and men would be desperately needed by her husband and the tenants. She told them that, thanks to Betty's nephew Ewell, Jamie was now safe and had been declared heir to the Arlington Estates. She told them that her mother's health had returned and that Jamie was fortunate to have so many loved ones to see to his welfare. Katherine explained that her mother was aware of all the arrangements

176

Katherine had made with the Mellons and that her mother looked forward to meeting them and sharing the joys of their grandson Jamie. Marie and Jamie had developed a wonderful relationship. In many ways Katherine's mother was a new and better person for having suffered all that she had. She seemed more self-reliant and sure of herself than ever. She was perfect with Jamie, loving, yet firm in her expectations that he would respect her and she him.

Katherine had added more servants to the staff at Whitehall. She wanted Arthur and Roberta to slow down some. Of course they were insulted at first, but she convinced them that they had earned the right to slow down and to have some free time of their own. She had hired a tutor for Jamie, a young man whom she had liked immediately. She thought that perhaps it would be good for Jamie to have more time in the company of a man, since there were so many women doting on him. Susan would continue to work with him, even after she and Carlton were married. If he still needs me by then, she had said. Jamie still had not spoken, but Susan planned, after her marriage, to cut down on her work with other children, so she would have more time for Carlton and Jamie. He was such a beautiful, happy child, they would accept him and be thankful for him if he never spoke.

Katherine had also written to Payton's family of the massacre and of her plans to return to Virginia about the first of July. She told William that the "Katy Two" was being made ready for her trip and that there would be room if he should decide to go with them to the colony. "I know it would lift the spirit of Payton to see his father and have the misunderstandings between you resolved," she wrote. She then went on to say that although he had not said so in his letter, this last massacre had left him wounded, in body and in spirit.

While Katherine was writing to the Montgomerys, Jamie came to her room and sat watching her. When she sealed the letter she told him that she had written a letter earlier, to his grandparents, telling them that she and Jamie hoped they would soon move to London. She decided this as good a time as any to tell Jamie that she was going back across the ocean because Payton needed her. She told Jamie that she knew he would be fine, with so many loved ones around to care for him. When she got back to the colony, she promised, she would write letters to him. Maybe before too long, Payton, the new baby and she would come back and see him. Or maybe he could come to Virginia when they got their new house built. Katherine told him she would like for him to work well for his new tutor and with Susan. "I love you Jamie and I fervently hope that by the time I return or you come to me, you will be able to tell me that you love me too."

Jamie stopped her then by putting his hand to her mouth; then he put both hands to her face, holding her attention as he a mouthed the words, "I love you."

Katherine was so surprised she could hardly answer him. She held him to her and said, "No matter how many babies I have you will always be my special child." She thought it best not to make too much of it in front of him, but she knew this was a real milestone. She couldn't wait to tell Susan.

By the end of June, the ship was ready and Katherine could think of nothing but getting back to Payton and seeing that his son--she always thought of the babe within her as a son--was born at Montgomery's Hundred, even though there was not much left there to call home. Dan had been wonderful in the organization of men and supplies for the trip. There were modern tools he said would make things easier, and he was now excited about returning. She had asked him to find a bricklayer if possible because she would feel safer in America with a home made of brick. She had asked him if there was any reason why the soil there would not make good brick, and he had told her the soil in certain areas was fine for brick. A few days before they were to set sail, he had found a bricklayer and the son who assisted him. They were both willing to go if they could take their families.

On the Katy Two, the cannon holds were now small compact cabins. Most of the families would have a cabin of their own. Even though crowded, they were better off than many who made the trip, including Katherine and the girls who had been with her on her first trip across the sea. Katherine's cabin was the one formerly intended for the captain, but she had arranged for him to have a comfortable cabin, situated just as well and which she had furnished with appropriate furniture. She planned on living in her cabin with the baby and Payton, until comfortable shelter could be built. The ship would carry many pieces of furniture from the smallhouse that had belonged to her maternal grandparents and now held special meaning for her. She had packed utensils and linens and many things from the smallhouse that would make their home in the colony more comfortable. She knew that the Mellons would want their own things around them in the common rooms. Roberta had helped her shop for nonperishable foodstuff, and Cooke Della had provided her with cured and preserved foods from the pantries of the smallhouse and the house at Whitehall. Katherine had gone down to the kitchen several mornings and listed the ingredients that Cooke Della used in some of Katherine's favorite dishes, with Cooke calling them off to her. There was so much she wanted to take for herself and the other women in the colony to make their jobs easier and life more pleasant. Dan groaned and complained every time she ordered more crates to be loaded on to the ship.

The night before they were to sail Carlton and Susan dined with Marie, Katherine, and Jamie. Carlton had mentioned before that it would be useful and likely profitable if Payton could provide and staff the shipping firm with a small office in the colony. He now had everything together in the way of forms and paper goods to open such an office and had found room for them on the ship. He was so excited about it that Katherine told him she would see to it herself, if Payton had no interest in it. Dan had been so good at organizing and seeking new tenants, she felt confident that the two of them could get it done. Carlton had become knowledgeable on shipping and felt the colony offered

179

opportunities for trade that were unavailable to England. As the colony grew it would double their business.

Marie and Susan were terribly concerned for Katherine, as she was now about six months along in her pregnancy. They worried that the baby might come before she reached America or that Katherine might have complications. Katherine tried to calm their fears by reminding them that seventeen wives were among the tenants going with her. Surely they would be able to take care of her. She did admit that she would rather be in Virginia when it was born, so that Molly could be in charge of her care. She told them how Molly had proven to be the most capable in the colony and was often called upon to go to other plantations in time of need. She seemed to have a sixth sense about those who were likely to have trouble and made herself available to them when their time came. Once, while helping Katherine with her bath, Molly had told Katherine that she was built well for child-bearing.

Katherine had covered everything that Dan and she could think of for their trip back. With sailing day upon them she resigned herself to releasing further worry and decided that anything undone would have to remain undone. She settled into her comfortable cabin, intent on beginning a course of study that would help to fill the long days of sailing and perhaps give her a philosophy with which she could she could live and grow spiritually. She had visited the stationers' shops in London and collected books she thought Payton and Reverend Moore would enjoy, books she intended to read on her journey. By the time she reached the colony she hoped to have clarified her contradictive beliefs concerning God and the church, Catholicism versus Protestantism and somehow integrate these with the humanist beliefs that had so appealed to her since her years in France. Having put England behind her and with the colony so far away, she would take this time to look within.

Chapter 23

The days at sea had now become long and Katherine's body had expanded so that there was no comfort in sitting, standing or lying. The aching tiredness in her back was with her constantly and she longed for the sight of land and for the sight of Payton. Her studies in spirituality had helped her to better understand all that Reverend Swann had tried to teach them and she knew that the safety of her child and her husband was in the hands of a power greater than human minds could imagine. Whenever she began to doubt that power, she immediately called a halt to her thoughts. It had become clear to her that when Jesus said that it is done to you as you believe, he was telling us that our thoughts and beliefs have the power to bring us the good we desire and that our fears and doubts can abort that good even when it is close at hand. During her time with the others on board Katherine had told them of Reverend Swann and his teachings; she had tried to explain to them how much more secure and how much closer one could feel to a God of love and principle. If they could only let go of their fear and open their minds to a new way of seeing, they would find that the real truths are imprinted on the hearts and souls of every one of God's beloved. She tried to explain that as we re-discover the truths they resonate with those imprinted on our soul, assuring us that our Creator is a God of love. Katherine could see that some of them immediately put a wall between themselves and her words. They were so afraid of questioning or examining their beliefs. In pondering their reactions she wondered if it was only when tragedy had left one with nothing, that one was willing to seek the truths within. Finding it hard to accept tragedy as the only way to truth, she prayed for divine guidance, the sentence that came to her was, "lest ye become as little children." It was then that she understood that we all come here knowing truth and then through our own misunderstandings and those of our teachers we are led astray. A philosophy that leaves one afraid to hear any other cannot be a secure philosophy. To become as little children would mean that we become inquisitive and open, expanding our understanding. With this sudden insight, she put her hand on her stomach and whispered,"Little child, you shall lead me."

After two days and nights of high winds and turbulent waters, the passengers aboard the Katy Two awoke on the morning of September 24, to find that, during the night, they had drifted into the quiet waters of the Chesapeake Bay. Katherine, having been brought from her bed by their shouts of joy, stood now at the rail with Dan and Melinda. Dan was telling Melinda that Chesapeake was an Indian word for "Mother of Waters." As they moved past the capes and entered the James River, Katherine thought of the line from Michael Drayton's ballad,"Virginia, Earth's Onely Paradise." She now knew that earth's only paradise was not a place outside ourselves. Jesus and other great spiritual teachers had come to tell us that heaven is within and that we don't have to wait till the end of our life on earth to experience paradise. When we convert to the pure, loving, accepting, nonjudgmental state of our childhood, paradise will be wherever we are. She, Dan, and Melinda held hands and formed a circle. With heads bowed, they each offered a silent prayer of thanks to the God who had guided them safely through the storm. After having spent so many of her days at sea reading, pondering, praying and listening to a higher wisdom she was more aware and more grateful for the gifts of God. She now gave thanks for the baby who moved inside her. She affirmed its safe keeping within her until the time was right for it to be born on the land of its father. The early high tide carried them swiftly along the James River and though the little ship slowed down when the tide started out, they still reached the crude wharves of Jamestown a little after dark. Most of the new arrivals on the ship wanted to stay at Jamestown for the night. Some wanted to look up family, friends, or acquaintances they had not heard from since the massacre. Other's were curious about the town and its people. Katherine thought it best to let them take this time before moving the ship on to Montgomery's Hundred. She wanted their new tenants to be at peace and ready to get to work when they reached what was left of their plantation. Dan, anxious about his family, had volunteered to take a smallboat on the morn and row to Montgomery's Hundred. Katherine prepared a note for Dan to give Payton. The bricklayer's son and Dan had formed a strong friendship; he wanted to go with Dan, so they set out at daylight.

The tobacco crop at Montgomery's Hundred was mature and had been hung to cure in the makeshift tobacco barns. They had done as well as could be expected, considering the shortage of men and tools. Payton knew that none of them would make a lot of money, but all of them would make some. The massacre had set them back and put them heavily into debt. There was little joy to be found among the people of his hundred, yet it was one of the most well-off of any. Living together in the longhouse and sacrificing everything for the crops was robbing them all of the spirit to go on. Payton, especially, showed the strain of the past six months. The few men left on the hundred, had worked with him from dawn to dusk. The gash on his upper arm was not yet healed. It had become infected, time and again. He worked with it throbbing and laid awake at night with it throbbing. Yet the throbbing of his arm did not compare with the ache in his heart. They had been reduced to living as heathens and though he longed endlessly for Katherine, he could not bear the thought of her living in such squalor. They had not time or energy for anything but their food crops and the tobacco. Starvation and disease had hovered at their door since March. Payton knew that the same battle raged in the mind of everyone there, whether to stay and fight for their dream or take what little each of them would receive from their tobacco, and, avoiding as many of their creditors as possible, get out of the colony before winter set in. It was somewhere toward the end of September, Payton guessed, as he lay on his pallet into the night with his constant companion, the smell of smoke. The clothes he had been able to salvage from the house were permeated with the black streaks and the burned-in smell of smoke. It was not the pleasant smell of campfire smoke; it was more like the sickening smell of a smoldering garbage heap. The long house and most of the possessions that the tenants had salvaged reeked of that smell also. Dominant over the smell of unclean bodies and sweat, it could not be escaped. Except on rainy nights like tonight, he slept outside, but the smell hung there too. The only place he could escape it was when naked in the river. Just before dawn he dozed off. Molly, aware that he had not slept and that he had become dangerously run down, insisted that he be left to sleep for awhile when daylight came. He would be angry with her but she knew he had just about pushed himself to the limit.

It was on that morning, the 25th of September, that an unknown man came with a message for Payton. Molly was told that the man had come with Ben's son Dan, on the ship they had heard was on its way up river yesterday. The man stood now, with a sealed paper and waited for Payton to be awakened from his pallet on the hard-packed dirt floor. When Molly approached Payton, she found him already awake. He told her he would be out in a few moments and she went to tell the man waiting.

There was a crispness to this September morning that, in years past, had inspired in Payton a zest for life. On this morning, awakening had brought with it, only a memory of zest, then the lethargy that had been with him for too long reclaimed him. Payton had seen better men than himself destroyed by the languor of hopelessness. After Molly had come to announce the messenger, he couldn't imagine any news being good news, so he took a moment to get his thoughts together before getting up. He rolled out and got on his knees beside the pallet, as he did every morning. He wanted, on this morning, to prepare himself for whatever news this messenger had brought. Payton did not believe in speaking to God in a begging, pleading tone. In fact, he thought it showed a definite lack of faith when one felt that they must continue to beseech and beg. He spoke his word for strength, affirming that, through the mighty power of God within him, he was equal to anything this day could bring. He quickly added an amen as he heard footsteps approaching. A young

184

man, whom Payton knew not, stood outside surrounded by the ever curious onlookers. Payton recognized her handwriting as soon as he saw his name and he felt a quickening inside.

"Dear Payton," it began, "In a very short time your babe will be born. We have traveled far that it might be born on its father's land. I fear that I have been extravagant with the dowry that was to come to you as my husband. So extravagant that I had to acquire my own ship to carry the purchases. I have purchased supplies and materials to begin the rebuilding of Montgomery's Hundred. I have transported seventeen new families to help with the rebuilding. We brought animals and food to help get us through the winter. Potter Ben's son Dan was a big help in recruiting new tenants and advising me on the purchase of necessities. The luxuries I chose on my own. Please hurry and come to me at the Jamestown harbor where I wait for you."

Payton took a moment to absorb the full meaning of the message and then to thank God for these unexpected blessings. He tried to gain his composure before looking up with glistening eyes at the ragged group who seemed braced for another blow. For almost six months they had lived and worked as one. This message was as much for them as it was for him. Reverently, he read the words into the stunned silence; then amidst the cheers and tears, Payton cleared his throat, swiped eyes and nose with ragged sleeve, and read the message through again.

The Payton who walked up the ramp in Jamestowne was not the same man who had first appeared before her. He had neither the finery nor the arrogance of that man. Yet he aroused in Katherine feelings even more powerful than the man that he had been. Here was a man who had suffered and had grown through his suffering. Here was a man who now understood what was truly important in life.

Heavy with child, but dressed richly in clothes made for the lady-in-waiting, she watched him approach with a feeling of uncertainty, looking to him for a cue as to the appropriate greeting. Katherine glowed with an inner beauty, a healthy shine that women often acquire when with child. To Payton, at that moment, she was an angel of light, representing all that is truly good and wholesome and worthwhile in life. Indeed, she was all the things he had feared never to see again. He opened his arms and she shot forward into them. Her healing energy flowed through him. Her love unified the fragments of his spirit and in that moment he knew wholeness. He inhaled her scent and it conjured up all the passion of one long ago night. She put a warm hand in his and whispered, "Let's go to my cabin."

On Michaelmas Day, September 29, 1622, Matthew Payton Montgomery was born aboard the Katy Two, moored in the James River at Montgomery's Hundred. Reverend Swann had suggested that everyone envision Katherine, the baby, and Molly as being surrounded by God's protective light throughout the process of birth. Now Mother and babe were resting peacefully in the capable hands of Molly. A Molly, whom Katherine had noticed, was now fully aware and mindful of everything around her. Molly had been pleased to hear of conditions with Jamie and thought maybe he had found his rightful place in the world. Dan's family were ecstatic to have him back, and had been celebrating the addition of his wife and her family.

The letter Katherine brought Payton from his father made Payton break down and cry. He assured her they were tears of joy, and thanked her, time and again for visiting them and for taking Jamie to meet his grandparents.

'Twas said that Payton had such a bighead over his son, that nary a one of them fancy hats that Katherine brought him from London would fit. There was a new sense of pride among the tenants of Montgomery's Hundred. They were proud of Katherine, the baby, and all that had begun to happen at their plantation. Ever eager to brag, they were, that bricks were being made and fired right there on their hundred and that framing had begun for what would be the first brick house in the colony of Virginia. 'Twas Lady Montgomery's desire to have a brick home, with tenant houses of brick to follow. 'Twas the Lady Montgomery's desire that her family, tenants included, be as safe as they possibly could be if another Indian uprising came. When the first bricks were laid to form the cornerstone of Lady Montgomery's house, 'twas said she was there with babe on her hip. "Halt," 'twas said that she said. "Let every eye see this cornerstone and know that we, as freeborn Britons, have come to Virginia to stay. We have brought with us our love of liberty. Know ye that our children and our children's children will create a government here that treats all men with equality, regardless of their station in life, their culture, their color, or their religion."

Preview of Author's Next Book

A Coat for a Soldier

By

Polly McCanless Kent

Camille Hutchinson saw that her hired carriage was approaching her home on Chestnut Hill. She could not imagine why two of Washington's soldiers would be coming out of her front door. From a pocket on the canvas bag which carried her music books, she took coins to pay the driver. Once the carriage had stopped and the driver had helped her down she hurried to see what this was about. The soldiers had reached the sidewalk and were coming toward her. The one in front stepped forth, his hand out in introduction. "Miss Hutchinson, I am Captain Morrison and this is Private Johnston. Early this afternoon we found one of General Washington's carriers on the road between Boston and Philadelphia. The man had suffered some violent blows to the back of his head and was unconscious. We suspect the Tories were after the information that he carried for they took all his papers. The only identification we could find on him was your name and address on the torn lining of his collar. We are on urgent business for General Washington but we couldn't leave one of our own there to die."

"Sir, are you saying you have taken a man into my home and left him there? I know of no one in Washington's army. I can't imagine how you came up with my name and address. You cannot leave him here."

"Miss, we have already wasted valuable time. We brought him here on a make-do stretcher that fell apart as we traveled. Philadelphia has one of the best hospitals in the country so we

188

must leave it to you to contact them and have him moved, if indeed you do not know him. Many lives depend on us reaching Washington's quarters before he moves out tonight. When I speak with General Washington, I will see what I can find out about this man and see that you get the information. You may then pass it on to the hospital if he is still there. We bid you good day, Miss Hutchinson."

Camille watched in stunned silence as the two rode away. What more could she have done considering the urgency of their business? Inside she found Roxie, her downstairs maid, had allowed the man to be put in the small study that had been turned into a bedroom for her father before his death. Thinking the man to be of some kin to Camille, Roxie had called in Jason to strip off the bloody clothes which now lay in a pile on the floor. In clean white nightshirt, the golden haired man now lay on his stomach as Roxie and Jason applied salve and bandages to the cleansed gashes on his head and neck. Camille picked up his coat and seeing the bloodstained lining of the torn collar she recognized the coat as one she had made about two years ago. At that time General George Washington had put out a plea for the women of America to make coats for his army. The women of her church had worked independently to produce one hundred and sixty coats, all made to the specifications given them. In order to add body to the collar and lapels of the coat that Camille made, she had cut up an old canvas music bag to use as a lining. Stamped on the bag had been her name and address, which now showed through the mangled fabric of the bloody collar.

Because it was near supper time and too late to send Jason, her manservant, to the hospital, Camille would send for Dr. Gorton who lived less than a mile away. Within an hour Jason returned with the doctor. After examining the man and stitching some of the gashes, Dr. Gorton explained to Camille that there was swelling in the brain from the blows and they could only wait to see if the man would regain consciousness when the swelling went out. When she mentioned that she intended to have him moved to the hospital the next day, Dr. Gorton began

189

shaking his head, "no." He then explained that due to an epidemic of yellow fever, even the corridors of the hospital were full of people, some dying because the hospital lacked the staff to give them the care they needed. "Should this man catch yellow fever, it would be fatal," he added.

About the Author

I was born Miladene McCanless, 10/24/41 in Mills River, NC. This is in the Western NC mountains, near Asheville. During the '40s the mountains were isolated from the rest of the world and being there was like stepping back in time. I felt very close to the customs and habits of the colonists because my parents were from Burnsville, a little town deep in the mountains where things had not changed much since the first settlers moved there. As a child I stayed there a lot with grandparents, aunts and uncles. I can't even remember them having a radio, so storytelling was the favorite pastime.

After I was older my father got wanderlust and we moved to Washington State, then to Northern California. When I was in High School, we moved back to NC. I have always expressed myself through writing and was encouraged by teachers to go on to college and study journalism. But, I fell in love, got married, went to cosmetology school and had three children by the time I was twenty-three. I did take creative writing courses and write during this time, even having things published in newspapers and small magazines. I have been a licenced cosmetologist since 1961 and owned beauty shops in NC and Florida. Working as a hairstylist gives one a lot of material for writing and keeps one in touch with what the general public is thinking and talking about. During the '70s I attended UNC-A, (University of NC, at Asheville), majoring in psychology. A divorce changed the course of my life and made me a single mother without the funds to continue so I did not get my degree. I have always taken advantage of community colleges and have never stopped taking classes. Fiction has always been my first love; to me that is where the real truths of life are found; facts and statistics change from day to day. People, and what they want from life for themselves and their children, change very little.

This book came about through a snip of information I read during the '80s in a magazine. According to court records in

England, it said, women were needed so badly in the colony of Jamestown they were being kidnaped and shipped to the colony. A Mr. and Mrs. Baley had been convicted of such kidnapings. This started a "what if" process in my mind that would not let me rest. I would get sidetracked for a year or two at a time, then the characters would start haunting me or another snip of information would come along and inspire me to get back on the story. I did research on this book three times because I lost it, once in a fire, once when moving.

I am ashamed to say that this book has been about eighteen years in the writing.

I think I have probably told you much more than you wanted to know so I will hush. You can e-mail me or call me and ask if there is more that you need.

To:

My wonderful Daughter Susan-

I Love You So Much:

For - being a wonderful Mother to My Grand daughter-

For - being A Great wife to our Son - in -Law-

For - being a loving Sister to your ~~Brother~~ & Sister-

For - Always being there for Your Dad & Me -

I hope your life will be full of Joy Always-

I Love You

Mama.